THE SCENT OF PROMISE

HEATHER REYBURN

For my Family

CHAPTER 1

Hannah Simpson increased her pace, her stride firm, her footfall soft.

I've done it. Finally! She crossed her fingers behind her back and waited to be admitted to the private office of the human resources department.

This was her chance. After two long years spent waiting in the wings, she was destined to win a position in the hierarchy of well-respected technicians and scientists instead of being the go-for, the jack of all trades but master of none.

Holding her head high and facing the closed door, she rubbed a foot against the back of her trousers, her nerves jangling. The door swung open.

"Please come in." The personnel officer stood back and smiled, her jangly earrings swinging. "Make yourself at home."

"Thanks, Karen." Hannah pulled out the chair opposite the officer's desk and nestled herself comfortably. The women faced each other and Karen sighed. A flash of alarm bit into Hannah and she shuffled forward, perching on the edge of her chair. Had she got this wrong? Was this not the promotion call after all?

Karen cleared her throat. "I'm sorry to have to inform you that you were unsuccessful this time."

Hannah's heart thumped in her chest. She rubbed her sweaty palms on her trousers. Staring at Karen, dumbstruck, she tucked her chin to hide the heat rising on her neck. *I don't believe this.* As shock morphed to frustration and then despair, she found her voice. "Can you tell me where I went wrong? Or why I'm unsuccessful?"

"Of course. You did nothing wrong. In fact, you scored extremely well. However, another of the candidates rated slightly higher and as you know, we must award the position to the highest-scoring applicant." Karen angled her head in obvious sympathy and Hannah blinked hard, her knuckles turning white as she clenched her fingers tightly together. "Do you have any other questions?"

Waiting for a few seconds, Hannah willed her tears to remain behind her eyes and not let her down. Drawing herself up in her chair, she asked, "Was the successful applicant a male?"

Karen stared at her for what seemed like a minute, the vein in her neck pulsing. Then she gave Hannah a silent nod.

Hannah rose to her feet and turned toward the door.

"I'm so sorry." The woman's softly spoken words followed her into the passage, penetrating her head, like a ghost she couldn't shake off. The stairwell door closed behind her with a loud click and she leaned on the handrail and gazed at her quivering hands. She took several deep, slow breaths, then proceeded down two flights of stairs. Pausing again on the landing outside her department, she lowered her shoulders and reefed the door open.

Questioning eyes seemed to bore into her as she slid through the door and calmly made her way to her desk at the far end of the room.

"Well, what's the verdict? Did you get it?" Ellie hissed the words, her face half covered with a hand.

Hannah met her gaze with a solemn stare. Her friend's beautiful Irish complexion had paled, and compassion softened her expression.

Hannah shook her head, her mouth tight. "No, apparently I scored well—but not well enough."

"Oh, I'm so sorry, Hannah." Ellie ducked around the partition and hugged her. "I really thought now that the old dog has gone, they would do their best to use a new broom. Lord knows that department could do with a good sweep—and there's no one more deserving than you."

Hannah pursed her lips. She agreed with Ellie—at least she had believed her hard work and innovative ideas would be welcome. *Apparently not.* "It looks like I'll have to keep on trying, Ellie, like I have for the last couple of years."

"Don't let it get you down. Look at the positives. Now you'll be able to concentrate on the Horse of the Year show and get that steed of yours leaping out of her skin."

Hannah shot her a rueful grin. Although not a horsewoman herself, Ellie loved animals and understood it required dedication and hard work to achieve a good rapport with a successful show jumper. She was right. The new job, had Hannah been successful, would have increased her workload and responsibilities, meaning getting time off to compete in her chosen sport would have been fraught with difficulty.

"How many weeks now?"

"Three." Hannah paused and glanced at the calendar above her desk. "Actually, it's less than that. Mum and Dad are coming down to watch and stay a few days so we can celebrate both Dad's and my birthdays after the competition."

"Fabulous. Let's hope that Hastings weather lives up to its reputation so you can pretend you're holidaying on the Mediterranean."

Hannah forced a brief smile on her face, compressing her disappointment deep inside until she could revisit it in privacy. She pulled her sleeve back and checked her watch. "It's nearly knock-off time. I'm going to leave a few minutes early so I can collect my jacket from Todd's before he gets home."

"Right. Sounds like a plan." Ellie's forehead creased. "I know you were together for four years, but I'm pleased you've seen him for what he really is—a narcissistic bully. You deserve so much better."

Hannah hugged her friend. *You'll never know how many times I ignored those red flags.* "Don't worry about me. I'm not made of porcelain. I'll be fine."

"I hope so." Ellie lowered her head and spoke softly. "You know I didn't believe you when you said it was your horse who gave you that black eye a few months back. It was Todd, wasn't it?"

Hannah shook her head as she grabbed her bag.

"Of course not. I told you it was my horse—and it was my fault, not hers." She leant across her desk and shut down her computer. Giving Ellie a small wave as she hurried out the door, she called back, "See you Monday."

CHAPTER 2

She pulled onto the main road, zig-zagging through the traffic as she made her way toward Todd's house, fighting back the traumatic memory of that ghastly evening. Taking slow, regular breaths, she struggled to cleanse her mind of the terror.

It was unfortunate that she'd knocked the bottle of wine over, but accidents happened. The problem was the newly laid and, as yet unsealed flooring.

Her pulse raced. The vision of bulging eyes and engorged neck veins as he'd lashed out still haunted her. *If he hadn't had so much to drink, I may well have been another statistic of domestic violence. Shame I forgot my jacket—but better that than being injured ... or worse.*

Approaching Todd's house, Hannah slowed and cast a glace around the neighbourhood. With no sign of life, she pulled into the drive and walked around to the back door. Plunging her hand into the peg basket hanging on the laundry door, she fished for the matchbox, removed the spare key, and slid it into the lock. After taking two steps inside, she reached up and lifted the wool jacket off the coat hook, then retreated as quickly as she had entered. Perfect for cool summer evenings and protecting her from the damp air of the Waikato, the beautiful jacket was her favourite and had cost half a week's salary the previous winter.

She locked the door behind her, stowed the key back in its hiding place, and dashed to the car. Wasting no time, Hannah reversed out and sped back to the highway. She glanced at the clock on her dashboard. *Phew, three minutes—and I'll never come back this way again.*

Hannah had never been more relieved to reach the shabby rental cottage on the outskirts of Cambridge. *How pathetic am I?*

As she swung into her driveway, her face softened. Her beloved horse, Afternoon Delight, was standing against the fence, her head hanging low and one front leg bent.

Hannah wound down her window and called to the mare. "You're a bit early for your dinner yet, girl."

She began her routine assessment of her horse, from head to hoof. Her smile faded. Delight's front leg was resting at an awkward angle, the toe of her hoof buckled under. "Oh my God." Her fetlock was firmly bound with electric fencing cord. Delight lifted her head, pricking up her ears.

Hannah switched off the car, leapt out, and hurried across the grass. "It's alright, girl. You're okay. I'm here now. Let's get you untangled." On closer examination, the wire appeared to be embedded in the mare's leg between the hoof and fetlock, almost hidden by dark blood stains on her black hair.

Glancing along the fence line, Hannah noted the broken section of cord farther down. Leaning over the wire, she listened for the tell-tale tick of electricity flowing through the wires before she attempted to climb through the fence. Nothing. *The line's probably shorting farther up because of the break*. Fighting panic, she bent over, slipped between the slack strands, and moved quietly toward Delight. Compassion for her beautiful mare vied with the fury rising within her. Keeping her voice low and calm, she vented to her horse.

"That bloody landlord. I agreed to allow him to repair the dilapidated fence with electric tape, not this treacherous cord stuff!"

Delight nickered softly, and Hannah stroked her ears, cradling her face against her chest. "Let's have a good look, hey?" She ran her hands over the horse's neck, talking soothingly to her as she moved down her shoulder and onto her front leg. The mare flinched as her fingers neared her fetlock, and Hannah sucked in a sharp breath. Blood oozed from her leg, dribbling over her hoof and onto the muddied ground.

"Oh no. We need a vet." She climbed back through

the fence, pausing only to grab her bag from the car and fish out the neat flip phone she had purchased just a month ago. Her previous red mini-brick version had met a sad end, thanks to Todd's jealous outburst following a conversation she'd had with a fellow show jump rider. Apparently, 'Todd's law' included the rule that any male friends, no matter how old or innocent their friendship, were completely inappropriate for Hannah.

"Please, please, pick up quickly." Relief flooded through her as the line clicked after only two rings.

"Good evening. Cambridge Equine Hospital. Jody speaking."

"Hi Jody. It's Hannah Simpson. I need help urgently please. My horse has her leg tangled in electric fencing cord and it's bleeding badly. Can someone come out?"

"Oh Hannah, that's bad news. Of course. Kevin's just got back from his last call. I'll send him straight over to you."

The familiar caring tones of her riding acquaintance eased Hannah's panic temporarily. She blew out a long breath, glancing down at her shaking hand and snapped the phone shut. Stroking the mare's nose, she whispered, "Help is coming. It'll be okay."

Hannah fastened Delight's headstall and tied her to the nearest post while she switched off the power-pack and continued the one-sided conversation with the mare. The fifteen minutes of waiting felt like hours before the familiar blue Subaru Forester drove down the driveway.

"Gidday, Hannah." Kevin threw the back hatch open and pulled a bag from the car before walking over to her. He climbed through the fence wires and studied the horse's leg, speaking quietly. "Hmm. You've made a bit of a mess of this one, haven't you girl."

Hannah's stomach cramped at Kevin's frown. "Bad news?" She focused on the wound. How had she been worried about a competition just an hour ago? Now her concern turned to whether her poor horse's jumping career may be over? Or worse? Her earlier excitement about the upcoming competition faded into oblivion.

"We'll give her a sedative first so I can get this wire off and have a good look at it." Kevin drew up fluid and slid the needle into Delight's vein before carefully unravelling the wire and mopping the blood from the mess of flesh.

Hannah bit her lip, barely daring to breathe as he inspected the wound. Tears prickled her eyes. *Why did that stupid idiot use cord?* With Delight's habit of pawing the ground while waiting for her evening feed, Hannah was certain the accident wouldn't have happened if the fence had been fixed properly. *Even if he'd used electric tape and run it higher up instead of hanging this thin rubbish thirty centimetres off the ground.*

Her head spun with worry and anger as she glared at the sheep in the next field. She loved the woolly creatures, but now she cursed them. *Not your fault. If your stupid owner fed you properly and didn't overstock your paddocks, you wouldn't be constantly trying to crawl under fences to get more grass.*

Kevin stood up and sighed. "I'm really sorry, Hannah. It looks like she's partially severed a tendon. It could have been worse, as you know. However, it's a serious injury and the healing process is usually quite slow. I'm afraid you won't be taking her to the Horse of the Year—not this time around, anyway."

A tear slipped down Hannah's cheek, and she swiped it away with the back of her hand. "What do I need to do?" She would not allow disappointment to overrule her love for her beautiful mare.

"I'll dress the leg now and show you how to redo it every second or third day. You'll need to keep her yarded." He glanced around the paddock. "Hmm, somewhere clean and dry if possible."

Hannah swung her gaze from his face to the churned mud around the fence lines and the heavy, poached surface at the gateway. "Well, this clearly isn't suitable. I'll ring around a few people I know and see if I can hire a stable."

"Good idea." He knelt down again and carefully cleaned the raw wound before spraying it with antiseptic and bandaging the leg from coronet to knee. "I'll give you some painkillers and anti-inflammatory powders to add to her feed each day and be back to check it again on Monday."

"Thanks Kevin. Thank goodness it's Friday. At least I'll have the weekend to organise something." She glanced toward her ute. "If I can't get anything better, my car can stay outside and I'll use the portable yards to set the carport up for her."

Kevin met her wry grin and harrumphed. "Could do worse. At least she'll be dry."

Hannah snorted. "Yeah."

While the Subaru drove away, Hannah turned back to her horse and let the tears slide down her face. She pressed her forehead against the horse's cheekbone and hugged her tight.

"I'm sorry, girl. It's not our turn for good luck this year."

CHAPTER 3

Hannah studied the vehicle shelter a few metres from her cottage. It was enclosed on three sides, and the roof was weatherproof and seemed secure. *What more do we need?* With renewed hope, she dragged the portable panels from inside her horse float and fastened one to each of the side posts with sturdy wire, tying them off with pliers and twisting the sharp ends to the outside of the posts, well away from a horse's reach.

She stood back and grinned to herself. "Thanks, Dad. Your lessons have been very much appreciated."

After slotting in the panel that joined the two together, she checked the latch, connected them correctly, and headed to the ramshackle garden shed that housed her lawn mower, wheelbarrow, and a stack of horse feed. A compressed bag of sawdust leaned precariously against the back wall. She had been saving it for bedding in the stable at their next competition. A pang of sadness flitted through her. *No point in thinking about it.* She dragged it to the carport and split the pack open, spilling the contents over the concrete.

"Perfect." She put her hands on her hips and inspected her work. A soft nicker drifted in the still evening air and her chest squeezed. "I'm coming, Delight. Won't be long." She mixed up chaff and horse nuts, added a drizzle of molasses, olive oil, and water, and tipped it into the plastic bin. Then she filled a large water bucket and placed it in the corner, peeled a biscuit of hay from the open bale, and returned to Delight.

Progress was slow as the horse hobbled beside her, barely able to touch the injured leg to the ground. Once inside the makeshift stable, her injury temporarily forgotten, Delight buried her nose in the food bin and began eating.

"Takes more than an injury to slow your appetite, doesn't it." Hannah sighed. Her heart ached as she reached for Delight's night rug. After buckling up the chest straps, Hannah pulled the soft fabric hood-and-neck-cover combination over Delight's head and clipped it to the D-rings on the sides of the body rug. Only the mare's ears, eyes, and nose were visible.

Hannah leaned against her neck, as Delight chewed. She brushed a hand along the sturdy rip-stop fabric on the mare's back. "We could probably leave all your clothes off for a while. You'd love that, wouldn't you?" She chuckled quietly, knowing Delight would take every opportunity to roll in mud if Hannah did just that.

Throughout the year, Hannah was fastidious about keeping her horse as clean and glossy as possible, and during winter, she added extra layers for warmth, depending on the weather. It was only when Hannah was grooming or riding her that Delight's rich dark coat, and black legs, mane and tail were exposed to the elements—something Hannah's mother, Dawn, had always found ridiculously amusing.

Leaving Delight to finish her feed, Hannah meandered inside and filled the kettle. *I'd better ring Mum and Dad and let them know.* The ache niggled in the pit of her stomach as she allowed disappointment to consume her thoughts once more. *I was really looking forward to the Show—and to having them both watch us compete.* While always supportive, having to leave the farm for more than a few days took enormous organisation, and since her grandparents had passed away, John and Dawn could not always find someone to feed and care for the animals. During her teenage years and after, Hannah had grown used to driving herself to Pony Club, horse shows, and competitions, with only her fellow competitors to cheer her on.

She poured herself a cup of tea, microwaved the risotto leftovers from the previous night, and slumped on the couch. While the television murmured in the background, Hannah barely registered its existence. *What a day.* She'd failed to win the sought-after position at work. Her relationship with Todd was well and truly history—which was actually a good thing, even if it irked her. And now, her dreams of competing at an elite level in New Zealand's most coveted show jumping competition had disintegrated.

Tired and fed up, Hannah lay on the couch and let her mind drift. At some point, she must have dropped off to sleep as she woke with a start, taking a few seconds to register that the melodic tune playing was the ringing of her phone. She leapt to her feet and grabbed it from the kitchen bench.

"Hello?" She frowned as the voice on the other end snuffled and mumbled, as though talking through a handkerchief or attempting to speak with a heavy cold. "Is that you, Mum?"

"Yes. I'm sorry, darling. I couldn't put off ringing you any longer."

Dread pulled at Hannah and her already tumbling stomach formed a knot. "Is something wrong? What's happened?"

There was silence for a few seconds and Hannah was about to ask again when Dawn spoke so softly Hannah shut her eyes, as if to better concentrate on her mother's words.

"Your father's been diagnosed with pancreatic cancer. We've been told he doesn't have long." Her sobs snatched away any further words and Hannah remained standing, frozen to the spot as questions and denial whirled in her head.

"Are you sure? I mean, could the doctors have got it wrong?" She waited for her mother to speak again.

"No. He hasn't been well since Christmas really and has lost a lot of weight since you were last home. He's been exhausted, and we thought he'd been working too hard. Now there's no casual worker in the area, and he's only got me to help. Then he complained of pain and the doctor thought it might be gallstones. He sent him to Auckland hospital for a whole heap of tests and … we got the results today." Dawn burst into a fresh round of sobbing.

Hannah moaned. A choking sound gurgled from her throat as she slumped to the floor. She tried to absorb her mother's words as her mind drifted, consumed by visions of her beloved dad. Smiling, playing with her in the yard, swimming and skylarking together at their tiny private beach, and her perched on the front of his saddle before she had her own pony.

She sat upright again as clarity filled her. "Mum. I'm coming home. Home to Fantail Ridge."

CHAPTER 4

Hannah ran over her mental checklist once again. *What have I forgotten? Rent paid in advance. Landlord knows I'll be away for a month, so there shouldn't be any hassle there.*

Work. Hmm. She opened her laptop and sent Brian, her manager, an email, hoping he would respond or ring her before Monday.

By the time Monday arrived, Hannah had given the cottage a thorough clean and packed her meagre belongings, leaving only a few kitchen items, the lawn mower, and the horse feed that wouldn't fit into the float.

At seven o'clock, only minutes before Kevin was due to check on Delight, Hannah's phone rang and she flipped it open. Her insides jumped as Brian's name flashed on the screen.

"Hello?" she said.

"Hi Hannah. I hope I've caught you at a good time?"

"Yes. It's fine. Did you get my email?"

"That's why I'm ringing. I'm so sorry, Hannah—about everything. As you know, I had no say in the decision about who got Jim's job."

"I know, Brian. It doesn't matter anymore." Hannah paused. His approval for unexpected leave was far more important after her mother's news.

"Don't worry about work, Hannah. Your family has to come first, and you must go home and support your parents now when they need you most."

Breath whooshed from Hannah, and her head spun with relief. "Thanks, Brian. I'll let you know what's happening once I'm home and can see for myself."

"Hannah, do whatever is needed. We'll miss you, of course—but I'm sure you won't miss us." He chuckled, and Hannah grinned at the phone.

"I'll be in touch," she said.

"All the best."

She snapped the phone shut. *Perhaps Brian has had something similar happen in his family?*

While she slathered butter and jam onto a piece of toast, Hannah dialled the real estate agent and waited until the ringing stopped and it clicked over to the answering machine.

"Hannah Simpson here. I'm going to be away for a while and have prepaid my rent for both this month and next. Please advise the landlord that I have my horse with me due to an injury caused by his poor fencing. While the paddock is empty, please ask him to make repairs—properly this time." She paused for a second and drew a breath. "You have my phone number if you need to contact me. Thanks."

Minutes later, Kevin arrived and redressed Delight's wound, seeming pleasantly surprised by the progress in less than three days. "Must be your nursing skills, hey?"

Hannah gave him a small smile and shrugged. "So … any instructions from here on?"

"She's a good traveller, isn't she?"

"Yes. She's the best. Had to be, I guess. We've covered a fair few miles together."

Kevin stroked the mare's cheek softly. "Good. If you can keep her movements to a minimum and dress her leg as we've just done every two to three days, I'm happy to give her the 'all clear' to travel."

Hannah grinned and led Delight to the tailgate of the float. Eager to hobble aboard, Delight reached for the hay net and snatched a mouthful of lucerne. "See what I mean? No trouble at all."

"Right then. Send me regular progress reports, Hannah, and I'll see you both again when you get back." Kevin bent to pick up his equipment while Hannah closed the bum bar and latched the ramp behind Delight.

"We're going home, girl. You'll have the stable and a nice clean yard for yourself, and your old friends will be there to welcome you."

Then she followed the vet down the drive and out onto the main road.

———

HANNAH WAS SURE THE TRIP HOME HAD NEVER TAKEN this long before. She gripped the steering wheel fiercely as her frustration grew. More cautious than usual because of Delight's injury, she had kept her speed down and been content to stay in her lane. Towing a horse float through city traffic was never a pushover, but today, the Auckland motorway seemed busier than usual, and, spying a gap in the traffic, she planted her foot on the accelerator and pulled out to overtake the truck in front of her.

"Hang on, girl. We're taking on the big fellas."

Half an hour later, the Helensville exit appeared ahead, and she breathed a sigh of relief. As she eased into the left-hand lane, the traffic lessened and she relaxed as they approached familiar countryside, allowing the soft rolling hills and long straight sections of road to soothe her. Memories flooded back of she and her father riding around the farm together, of her standing on his shoulders as a child and leaping into the water on hot summer days, and she fought the tears that threatened to fall.

———

TAKING LONGER THAN USUAL, HANNAH CAREFULLY reversed the float as close to the house paddock at Fantail Ridge as possible. She had untied Delight and was lowering the tailgate when her father's voice called out.

"Hello, love. Let me give you a hand."

Her head jerked around and she ran the few metres to him, wrapping his thin body in her arms and pressing her face into his shirt collar to hide her shock. In a few short weeks, her strong, healthy dad had faded to a shadow of his former self. It was not only the weight loss, but the colour of his skin, which was now a pale shade of grey while his previously clear eyes were tainted yellow. Hannah brushed her hand over his once thick, curly hair and held him tight. She swallowed hard and released her grip, meeting his sky-blue eyes—a mirror image of her own.

"Dad." Her voice caught in her throat and she choked back tears. "Sh-should you be outside?"

He chuckled and squeezed her gently. "I can do whatever I feel like, according to the doctors. Your mother's in the shower, so let's get this horse of yours settled into the stable before she appears."

Hannah forced a stoic grin on her face and swung her gaze back to the float where Delight remained, waiting patiently for the cue to reverse out. She unlatched the bum bar and flicked it to the side. "Back off, girl." The mare hobbled slowly, taking small steps, hopping on her good front leg while the injured limb hovered off the ground.

"Crikey. She's in a bad way, isn't she?" The creases across John's forehead deepened, and Hannah nodded.

"It's been a pretty awful few days for her." She picked up the lead rope while her father opened the gate into the paddock. As the smallest field on the farm, it had housed the chook pen, milking bail, and dog kennels since 1935. Now, it included two solid stables, each opening into a neat, square yard. Next to the stables, a concrete slab led to a tack room and wash bay for the horses, providing ample storage for the many saddles, bridles, rugs, and equipment that Hannah and her dad had accumulated over the years. Halfway down the paddock, they had installed a levelled arena filled with a mix of sand and sawdust, completing the conversion from the original house cow and chicken compound to a small but efficient horse facility.

"I've put plenty of bedding in the stall so she'll be comfortable," her father said as he latched the gate behind them.

Hannah could barely take her eyes off her father's stooped back as he shuffled carefully in front of her. Her chest tightened, and her breath caught as tears welled again. Since the age of thirteen, she'd been tall—but she had never considered for a minute that one day she would be taller than her father.

The water trough was full, and fresh hay filled the

mesh rack. "Leave her to it now, love, and come and have a cup of tea." John reached for Hannah's hand and they returned slowly to the house.

The small gate clicked and Dawn rushed toward them, her arms outstretched. "Welcome home, my darling."

Hannah dropped her father's hand and hugged her mother, releasing her breath in a long, shuddering sigh. After the heartache of the past few days, it was good to finally come home.

———

AFTER DINNER, HANNAH AND HER MOTHER SAT IN THE armchairs, their legs raised on footstools, while John stretched out on the couch. Snuggled under a soft tartan rug despite the mild evening, he dozed while the women talked.

"How's Bestefar?" Hannah asked.

"He's marvellous. Still pottering around in his shed and tending his bees. He'll be thrilled to see you. Did I tell you he's excited about receiving a telegram from the Queen soon?"

"Yes, Mum, you said he's told you a few times. I suppose it's pretty exciting turning a hundred." Hannah shared a small smile before her gaze rested on her father. *Why couldn't Dad have a few more years?*

Hannah had expected Ed, her pseudo grandfather, to be the next death after his sister, Hilde, and

Hannah's paternal grandparents. With no family of their own other than each other, Ed and Hilde had both adored and mentored Hannah throughout her childhood. As native Norwegians, they had encouraged her to call them Bestemor and Bestefar in the Norwegian tradition, and when Hilde had passed away, she'd left an enormous hole in Hannah's life.

Staring at the television screen, Hannah brushed away the stray tear that trickled down her cheek. Pushing herself out of the chair, she said, "I'm going to make us a warm drink. Do you think Dad would like something?"

John gave a slight flick of his wrist and moaned softly.

"It's alright, dear." Dawn turned to Hannah and shook her head. "It's time for me to give him medication now and get him settled."

The ache deep inside her spread slowly to her limbs and by the time the kettle boiled, Hannah couldn't pour the hot water into their cocoa. *It's not fair. Dad doesn't deserve this horrible illness. He's the best father a girl could ever want.*

She wanted to punish someone, to rant and rave about the futility and injustice of it all—but she did neither. Instead, consumed with frustration and sorrow, she slid to the floor and, with her back against the cupboard, she covered her face with her hands and sobbed quietly while her mother put her father to bed.

———

WHILE JOHN SLUMBERED, HANNAH AND HER MOTHER returned to the kitchen where they sat sipping hot cocoa and alternately talking and crying until late. As an only child, Hannah was grateful for the strong bond they had always shared—one more like sisters than mother and daughter. The physical likeness between Hannah and her mother was strong. They shared thick, curly hair, fair, freckled skin, and a wide mouth that tipped up at the corners. However, she had inherited the sapphire-blue eyes of her father and grandfather, along with a powerful love of the farm and animals. While she welcomed her father's easy-going temperament, Hannah was thankful she had inherited some of her mother's strength and forthrightness, even when it got her into trouble on occasions. In tough situations, she had called on it—like when her beloved Border Collie had died of old age, her 'best' friend had stood by and watched her being bullied during their first year at high school, and when Todd's attempts at manipulating her became too much.

But her father's illness was tougher than she could ever have imagined.

Clinging to each other, she and Dawn hugged as though they were drowning. Dawn stroked Hannah's hair until their tears dried and they could cry no more. Eventually, they parted and collapsed on the couch.

Hannah reached into the drawer under the coffee

table and fished out a hairbrush, then passed it to her mother. She slipped to the floor and nestled against Dawn's legs before pulling out her hair tie and shaking out her auburn locks. Then she closed her eyes as her mother began brushing the thick hair. The ritual was as comforting as ever—a practice that Dawn had maintained since Hannah was a young child.

"Come and sit on my knee, Scruffy."

The little dog hauled himself out of the squishy bed, narrowly missing stepping on the ancient tabby cat they called Ragamuffin. He squirmed his way onto Hannah's lap, turning in a circle before flopping down with a groan. Of dubious breeding, he had joined the family ten years before, when Hannah had come home after completing her science degree, bringing the tiny pup with her as a gift for her mother's fiftieth birthday.

At the memory of her handsome, adoring father standing next to her mother while she cut her birthday cake, tears once again ran down her cheeks.

As Dawn's gentle strokes became slower, the rhythmic motion of brushing less urgent, Hannah let her chin drop to her chest and closed her puffy, exhausted eyes.

———

HANNAH SLEPT FITFULLY DESPITE THE COMFORT OF THE familiar bedroom surroundings and Ragamuffin's rhythmic purring against her back. Slipping quietly out of bed, she dressed as the early morning sun threw pale golden rays into the sky. She slid the heavy kitchen door open, stepped into her gumboots, and strolled into the courtyard. Roses climbed the trellis behind the bright palette of petunias, their fragrance drifting on a breeze so gentle it hardly kissed her skin. Tubs of red geraniums lined the wall of the old shed, and fuchsias a metre high filled the gap on either side of the door to the shearer's room. Hannah smiled at the flowers. Like tiny dancers, the fuchsia flowers had always been her favourite, their pink and purple skirts mimicking a ballerina's tutu.

Hannah pushed the gate open and, with Scruffy at her heels, strode to the stables. A nicker welcomed her and Delight poked her pretty head over the door, watching Hannah's approach. After mixing a feed for the mare, Hannah removed the horse's rug and brushed her glossy coat.

The sun rose, casting warm rays over the paddock, and the corrugated-iron roof crackled as it absorbed heat.

"That should do you for now." Hannah waited while Delight licked the final crumbs from her feed bin.

While the horse nibbled her hay, Hannah leaned on the stable door and gazed around the paddock. Jet and Lass, the two farm dogs, sat outside their kennels facing her, their ears pricked.

"I suppose you two want me to let you off for a run."

Hannah chuckled as both dogs leapt to their feet, their tails waving frantically.

She spent a few more minutes talking to her horse before striding toward the dogs and letting them both loose. She chuckled as they lolloped around her playfully then bounded toward the house.

"Go, Scruffy. You can do it!" The little dog, less than half their size and three times their age, raced ahead as though taunting them to catch him. Jet's Huntaway legs were gangly, reminding Hannah of a teenager struggling to control his rapid growth spurt. He stumbled in the long grass, while Lass, the black and white Border Collie, bounced half-heartedly behind him.

Hannah opened the house yard gate and all three dogs followed her to the boot room, sniffing Scruffy's empty feed bowl before returning their attention to Hannah.

"Stay, you lot. I'm just checking on Mum and Dad." The dogs obediently dropped to the floor and Hannah nodded. "Good dogs."

The kitchen was still and silent, and she frowned as she checked her watch. Eight o'clock. She filled the kettle and switched it on before padding softly down the hall to her parents' bedroom.

She opened the door. Her mother sat in bed ... reading? Hannah opened her mouth to speak, then closed it abruptly as Dawn put a finger to her lips. Casting a glance at the mound beside her, Dawn slipped out of bed and wrapped her dressing gown around her before propelling Hannah back toward the kitchen.

"He's had an awful night—the pain is increasing." Creases on Dawn's forehead deepened and Hannah grabbed the stone bench for support, it's cool, hard surface offering her familiarity.

"Really? Could it be affecting him that quickly?" Hannah stared at her mother's worried face. "He was only diagnosed a few days ago."

"I know, love. But he's probably had it for much longer than we realised. They warned us it's a very fast-growing form of cancer." Dawn's lip quivered and Hannah hugged her, desperately trying to understand why something hadn't been done before now.

"I think he's relaxed more now that you're home. We'll leave him to sleep for a while and get the chores done, then I'll see how he is." Dawn straightened her shoulders and shot Hannah a fleeting smile. "The district nurse will call to see him this afternoon some-time, so perhaps we could have a quick drive around the farm to check on things before she arrives."

Hannah poured their tea and nodded. "Will he be okay to leave?"

"Oh yes, he'll probably sleep."

"H-how long is it since Dad has actually been out to confirm all is well?"

Her mother shrugged silently and stared at her. "I'm not really sure. Perhaps four weeks. No, probably more, because it was before he started complaining about this pain under his ribs."

Drawing in a deep breath, Hannah re-tied her ponytail while thoughts ran riot in her head. As strong as her mother may have been, it was already clear that the farm was the least of her worries.

Hannah wished she could make her dad better, that there was something she could do—

But maybe there was. Perhaps, by keeping the farm running, she could free up her mother's time, allowing her to focus on her husband. It may even help John sleep better.

Yes. She would run the farm for the next two months. *It's over to me.*

CHAPTER 5

For the next two days, Hannah encouraged her mother to concentrate on caring for John and forget about the farm.

While she drove around the stock and checked fences and water troughs, making notes as she went, Hannah's heart sank. Clearly, it had been much longer than four weeks since her father had taken a serious look at things. Fly-strike affected a flock of older ewes. The unseasonably humid summer and many sun showers had kept the wool around their backsides damp enough to provide the perfect temperature for flies to lay their eggs—and now, maggots crawled through the warm, damp wool.

One hay paddock was still uncut. How on earth her father had found the strength to stack the hundreds of bales in the shed—or had someone helped him? She closed the doors carefully, leaning heavily on one as she tried to slide the bolt into the bracket.

"Blast. Another job." A hinge hung by a teetering nail. It had almost rusted through, and she knew that if her father had noticed it when he was filling the shed, he would have repaired it immediately. Alarm bells rang as Hannah came to terms with the fact that he was sicker than she realised—and had been for some time.

On the run-off, things appeared brighter. The cattle were fat and glossy and the calves growing well. *Probably too well*. Almost as big as their mothers, many of them were ready to wean—a job Hannah knew would take more than just her to manage.

Dad doesn't need to know.

Later that afternoon, Hannah ignored the pile of mail sitting on the office desk and retreated to the stables with the excuse that Delight needed attention.

She settled in the corner of a stall on the top of a rusted old bucket, her notepad resting on her knee. The familiar smell of horse and hay washed over her, and she loosened her grip on her pen. It would be okay. She would get this done.

All she needed was a little bit of help.

She pulled the list of phone numbers from her pocket and flipped her phone open.

After two fruitless calls to neighbours, Hannah panicked. On the third, Hugh Bennett, her father's old school friend and a near neighbour, answered.

"Hannah. Lovely to hear from you."

"Um. I was wondering if I could ask for some help, please?"

"Of course. What's up? Your dad still crook?"

Hannah froze. She hadn't considered that the Bennetts may not know the awful diagnosis and wasn't sure how to begin. Does Dad want people to know? "Yes. I'm home for a little while and would like to wean the calves, but Dad's not really up to it and Mum's busy too."

Hugh's jovial voice became serious and his tone softened. "Just name the day, Hannah, and both Andrew and I will be there. We'll need to be home for afternoon milking, of course."

"Thanks so much. I'll get back to you. Got a few fly-blown sheep to deal with first." She chuckled softly.

"No worries. We'll be on standby for you."

"Thanks, Mr Bennett. Goodbye."

She turned to Delight and rubbed her nose. "One problem down. Now we have to work out the next."

———

DAYS BLURRED INTO A FORTNIGHT AS HANNAH AND Dawn contrived a plan to accomplish the essential farm chores while making light of the work involved so John wouldn't feel responsible. As his health declined, every day became more difficult—some much harder than others.

It delighted Hannah when both her parents

appeared in the woolshed soon after she brought the flock of ewes in. Her father was having one of his better days and leaned on the yards while Lass kept the pens full under his guidance. Hannah methodically checked each sheep, drafting those that needed crutching into a separate pen. Then, for the rest of the day, she bent over each one, sweat dripping down her forehead as she pushed the electric handpiece through the wet, stinking wool around the tail. Dawn squirted antiseptic powder onto the raw wounds before briskly sweeping the offending wool aside while Hannah released the treated sheep and returned to the catching pen for the next patient.

"Phew. I thought I was fit, but I'm not." Hannah grimaced as the final sheep disappeared down the chute into the outdoor pen.

Dawn looked at her, an anxious frown on her face. "Are you sure you're okay to take them back to the paddock?"

"Yes, Mum. I'm fine. You look after Dad, and I'll be back as quickly as that old gentleman can carry me."

Hannah had caught Monty, John's aging gelding, and her own retired pony and installed them in the house paddock the previous day so they could talk to Delight over the stable rails.

She walked to the yard where the horse dozed in the afternoon sun. "Come on, old fellow. We can do this." Hannah patted the horse's thick neck, relieved that, in spite of his age, he bore little resemblance to the pathetically thin horse she and John had rescued from the sale yards many years before.

She slipped the bit into his mouth and pulled the headpiece over his ears. "Hmm, your teeth need filing, and you could do with an extra boost of nutrients, I think. If you help me finish our work, I'll get you sorted out so you get some of that energy back—just like when you first came to live with us."

He shook his head as if in agreement. She grinned and lifted the saddle onto his back.

———

WEANING THE CATTLE ON THE RUN-OFF WAS A SLOW task, and Hannah dithered over which horse to ride. Eventually she chose Honeysuckle to allow Monty to rest and adjust to his new diet. With Dawn and John in Auckland for yet another doctor's appointment, Hannah was resolute. She would have the job completed and be home again before they arrived back.

Honeysuckle valiantly cantered back and forth, leaping over ditches, and scrambling up and down the hills while Hannah called to Jet, encouraging his deep bark to flush out the cattle determinedly hiding behind scrub and misbehaving as much as possible.

The Bennett truck arrived as she was pushing the final cows into the yards, and she slid off the heavily sweating pony, brushed her face on her sleeve, and tied Honeysuckle under the shade of a tree.

"Thanks very much for coming. I appreciate your help," she said as Hugh and his son slid out of the truck in front of the loading ramp, the midday sun beating down on their tanned faced.

"No worries, Hannah. Any time." Hugh pushed his hat back and massaged his shiny scalp as he surveyed the bellowing cattle. "Yep, it certainly is time to get these great lumps of calves away." He grunted.

Aware they were in better shape than the dairy calves grazing in the Bennett's front paddock, Hannah wasn't sure if it was a rumble of disgust or envy.

———

RELIEVED TO BE HOME AGAIN, HANNAH RUBBED Honeysuckle down and gave her a special treat of pony nuts for tea. Then she hobbled toward the house.

Riding a fat pony with a short, bumpy stride wasn't quite the same as enjoying Delight's smooth, even paces, and Hannah grinned to herself. "You're going to have a sore rear end tomorrow, girl."

Showered and rehydrated, Hannah peeled a pile of vegetables and slid them into the oven with the leg of lamb as the late afternoon sun shone through the kitchen window. She snatched the blind and pulled it halfway down the pane.

"What time do you reckon Mum and Dad will be home?" She directed her words at Ragamuffin, who stared at the empty feed bowl in the kitchen corner.

"Oh, don't ignore me. I know it really doesn't matter. I'm tired and grumpy—that's all."

Meow.

Hannah gave an amused huff and pulled the box of cat biscuits from the cupboard.

Almost two hours later, Hannah was alternately slicing the meat and stirring the gravy when her parents' car puttered into the yard. She switched off the element and ran her hands under the tap. Tonight's dinner was to be special—a quiet meal to celebrate both Hannah's and John's birthdays with their favourite—roast meat and vegetables with gravy. For dessert, they would have apple pie and ice cream.

The gate slammed behind Dawn, and Hannah peered around her mother. "Where's Dad?"

Dawn shook her head silently. Her knees buckled. Hannah gasped and grabbed her mother's arms, steadying her.

"What's happened?"

"His blood count was low, and he was so weak they wouldn't let me bring him home. They'll give him a transfusion and set up a Niki pump before reassessing him. Only if he improves significantly will they 'consider' allowing him to come home."

"Oh, Mum." Hannah hugged Dawn tightly, then stepped back. "What's a Niki pump?"

"Apparently, it's a drip thingy that delivers continuous medication subcutaneously." She pressed her hand to her mouth. "They use it for palliative patients."

"Oh Mum. Does that mean …?" Hannah couldn't bear to finish the sentence.

"I don't know, love. I only want your father to be comfortable and out of pain." She held her hands up. "If that means he has to stay in hospital, then we have to accept it." Her shoulders heaved as tears trickled down Dawn's face and Hannah held her close, helpless to know what else to do.

———

A FEW DAYS LATER, HANNAH SAT AT HER FATHER'S hospital bedside, her hand resting in his, while her mother went in search of a hot drink for them both. While her father drifted in and out of consciousness, Hannah stared at the birthday card on his bedside table. His seventieth and her thirtieth birthdays had passed almost unnoticed, and a sadness consumed her —a numbness that pressed her into a pit of despair. The Horse of the Year competition would be over—and she did not even know the results. Would she and Delight ever get another chance?

She glanced at her father, his face almost as pale as the sheets. Who cared if it meant she didn't have any more time with him?

It had been more than a day since he'd attempted to speak and she was desperate for a word of recognition or acknowledgement.

Seconds later, his thin whisper reached her.

Hannah started. She leaned over him, holding her face close to his, frowning as she strained to hear.

Dawn walked through the doorway, and Hannah shot her an anxious glance.

"He's talking," Hannah whispered as her mother hurriedly placed two cups of coffee on the windowsill and bent over the other side of the bed.

"John. John, I'm here. I know you can hear me …" Dawn choked back tears, pressing her handkerchief against her mouth.

"I'm sorry. Really sorry." John's voice wavered, a thin murmur.

"Oh, Dad. Don't be. Please." A lump formed in Hannah's throat and she bit back tears. "You're the best father a girl could ever wish for. Thank you." Her voice cracked and her eyes met her mother's across the bed. Hannah reached out and pressed the nurse's call button while John's breathing grew silent. The only sound in the room was Dawn's quiet sobs.

"Mum. It's okay." Torn between comforting her mother and holding her beloved father's hand, Hannah dropped her head. His familiar work-roughened fingers had softened, the deep cracks and stains now barely visible. How had she not noticed before?

Hannah lay her head on her father's chest and let her silent tears soak the sheet, knowing that the words he had just whispered were his last.

CHAPTER 6

The following few days dragged as Hannah struggled to divide her time and energy between consoling her grief-stricken mother, funeral preparations, and running the farm.

Delight's leg had improved enough to allow her to graze in the small paddock during the day, relieving Hannah of having to feed and check her so often.

While fielding many phone calls, boiling the kettle twenty times a day in order to sustain the constant stream of visitors, and attempting to feed both the animals and her distraught mother, all thoughts of her job flew out the window. It was late at night, over four weeks after her homecoming and days since her father's death, when she remembered the date. She'd told Brian she'd update him on her situation after a month. Guilt gripped her, and she lay for a moment, forming an email in her head as a vision of her boss's kindly face flashed before her. She climbed out of bed, switched on her laptop, and waited for the internet to connect.

Hi Brian,

Apologies for not replying sooner.

My father passed away a few days ago, and I am currently arranging the funeral and attending to the farm, etc.

I will need more time here to sort things out but will email again in a day or two to provide an update. Sincere apologies for any disruption this is causing you and our department.

Kind regards,

Hannah

She drew a deep, shuddering breath and closed the laptop.

———

With a welcome surge of clarity, Hannah spent an hour on the phone the following morning discussing arrangements with her two uncles, George and Tim.

"I would like to deliver the eulogy, Hannah—if that suits you, of course." Hannah smiled to herself and switched the phone to her other ear as her Uncle George's deep, solemn tones echoed in her head.

"Yes, of course."

"And afterwards, perhaps you and your mother

would like to stay the night with us as we have quite a lot to discuss."

Hannah raised her eyebrows. What could there possibly be to talk about? The farm was owned jointly by both her parents. Surely her mother would now be the sole owner?

She shrugged. Uncle George had always been the serious one, with his accountancy background and position as eldest in the family. That seemed to allow him the right to advise and mentor the rest of the clan.

"Okay. The Bennetts have said they'll look after the animals if we want to stay in Auckland for a couple of days. See you tomorrow then." She paused, waiting for the inevitable harrumph that seemed to end all George's conversations. When it arrived, the shadow of a smile touched her lips and she hung up.

"Thank goodness for Aunty Suz and Aunty Jill," Hannah muttered as she unwrapped the bandage on Delight's leg. The deep cuts had healed well, the raw, bleeding flesh now replaced with healthy pink tissue. Delight bent her head and attempted to rub the freshly exposed skin. "Uh-uh. I know it's itchy, girl, but you're too rough. If you make it bleed, it will take twice as long to heal."

Hannah tightened the tether rope and deftly rubbed ointment on the new flesh before re-bandaging Delight's leg. Releasing the buckle on her headstall again, she patted the horse on the neck. "Away you go. Enjoy your freedom."

As Delight moved a few paces into the paddock, Hannah frowned. The injury may have looked clean and healthy, but the mare was still reluctant to put weight on her sore leg for more than a few seconds.

Hannah heaved a sigh. "I think we've got a long road ahead of us."

———

CROWDS SPILLED ONTO THE FRESHLY MOWN LAWNS around the Helensville church, and Hannah blinked in the bright sunshine as she stepped onto the path. With a soft smile plastered on her face, she stood close to her mother, relieved they had delayed the funeral for an extra couple of days as the steady stream of well-wishers hugged, shook their hands, and shared memories and sympathy. Earlier, inside the church, Hannah had glanced sideways at her mother, relieved to see Dawn smiling as Richard stood at the lectern and delivered his recollections of holidays spent on the farm with his uncle, aunt and beloved cousin, Hannah. His two brothers were busy travelling the globe, unable to attend.

But it didn't matter how far away they were— Hannah could feel the love shared by all her cousins. In the preceding days, both she and Dawn had wept buckets while they reminisced over good times and lost opportunities. Now spent, they were grateful for the love and support that surrounded them.

————

HANNAH LAY BACK ON THE SQUISHY CREAM COUCH, staring at the massive painting above the fireplace. Framed in an ornate timber and gold surround, the turbulent sea, clouds, and stark, lonely lighthouse seemed to echo her feelings and reach into her soul. Although her aunt and uncle's exquisite lounge room oozed charm and style, it was also comfortable and welcoming. Hannah slipped off her good shoes and closed her eyes.

She was exhausted. Guilty relief washed over her at the sound of her mother's voice in the kitchen, chirpy as she chatted with Hannah's aunties, Suz and Jill.

Thanks, aunties. You're the best.

Content to be surrounded by familiar, loving faces, Hannah was glad that Uncle Tim and Aunty Jill were also staying the night with Susan and George—making the most of the enormous guest suite and the vacant bedrooms. She missed sharing the company of her own generation. The catch-up with her cousins had been brief, but she understood Paul and Cara, George and Susan's grown-up offspring, had their own families to worry about. They had attended the funeral and stayed longer than most, enjoying the evening barbeque held at Aunty Jill and Uncle Tim's before she and her mother and her two aunts and uncles had driven to this gracious home in Remuera. It had been a long day.

"Are you ready, Hannah?" George's commanding

voice was gentle but firm and Hannah jumped, blinking rapidly.

"Y-yes, I guess so. What for?"

"If it's alright with you, I think it would be an appropriate time to discuss John's will and the farm accounts. Perhaps toss a few ideas around."

Hannah was suddenly wide awake, adrenaline heightening her uncle's puzzling comment. "I thought it was all cut and dried? Dad left his half of everything to Mum, just as they planned years ago."

"Hmm. Come, Hannah. We'll sit at the dining table so I can spread out the paperwork for you."

Hannah plonked herself next to George while her mother, Tim, and Jill sat opposite. Susan placed a mug of tea in front of each of them before taking her seat at the end of the table.

George cleared his throat and began. "I've asked Tim and Jill to join us as they may have suggestions or contributions that could help."

Hannah's anxiety and confusion grew. *What on earth is going on?*

"The first thing you need to know is that unknown to any of us in this room, John changed his will only weeks before his diagnosis, and Hannah, his half of the farm is now yours, not your mother's."

Hannah stared at him in shock, before swivelling her gaze to her mother. The possibility of her inheriting the farm after both her parents died was a given, but now? *What about Mum? Did Dad always expect me to come home if anything happened to him? Even if he did, surely he knew I had a life in Hamilton?* Dawn met her gaze, her face pale and still. *You didn't know either.*

"As you know, I have taken care of the annual taxation affairs for Fantail Ridge for over fifty years. During that time, I have offered my suggestions for management of profit and expenses to Mum and Dad when they were alive, and since then, John and you, Dawn." He nodded toward Dawn before glancing at Hannah. "My advice has not always been accepted." George stiffened before continuing. "So, what I am about to tell you is not good news."

Hannah's stomach did a somersault.

"Dawn, you remember that you and John refinanced after our parents died." Without waiting for her acknowledgement, he droned on. "Unfortunately, that was when interest rates were sky-high, so I recommended you repay only the interest each year, not the principle."

Dawn nodded and answered quietly. "Correct. It was a struggle to even do that for some years, but we had no choice. We had death duties to pay."

"Hmm. And there lies the problem."

Hannah's patience was wearing thin, and she couldn't help herself. "Please explain, Uncle George."

Tim caught her eye across the table and gave a wink, a glimmer of a smile playing around his mouth. She recognised the kindred spirit. *Get to the point.*

George harrumphed and rubbed a hand through his

thick, snow-white hair. "So the situation is, the farm now carries an enormous debt—one that I doubt you or your mother will service, Hannah."

"But can't we just sell some stock to get ahead a bit?" Hannah glanced at the confused, anxious look on her mother's face and shot her a reassuring smile.

"The problem is much greater than that. Land values have sky-rocketed in South Head, as they have in all areas within commutable distance to Auckland—thanks to the wonderful improvements in road construction. Although interest rates have come down, and your father reviewed the loan and locked in a lower rate, he ... well, he never got ahead again."

Hannah folded her arms and leaned her elbows on the table. "So, how big is the mortgage?"

"We're talking an amount greater than the value of the home farm, and possibly even including some of the run-off. Frankly, I am surprised the bank hasn't been in touch with you. If you cannot service the loan, they could foreclose."

"Really? Are you serious?" Hannah shuffled in her chair, clutching the table for support. She reached for her tea and gulped a mouthful, the scalding sensation leaving her numb.

A vision of letters with the bank's header on them flashed through her memory and guilt flooded her. They had been on the office desk and, with the worry of her father and Delight, plus the farm work, she had forgotten about them. *Were they something to do with the loan?*

"Yes, really. That's why I've asked Tim and Jill to be here. I believe it may be time to say goodbye to our childhood home and put the place on the market."

"Is it really that bad, George?" Tim leaned forward, deep creases forming on his brow. "Couldn't Dawn and Hannah apply to refinance? Or perhaps look at selling off one of the title deeds?"

Hannah studied her mother's pale face and realised how deeply the conversation had rocked her world. *Oh God, Mum. Are you able to understand the situation Dad left us in?* Hannah's head spun with options as she reached across the table and squeezed her mother's hand.

"Do you have the valuations for both properties, Uncle George?"

George rustled through the pile of papers and opened a spreadsheet, then laid it in front of Hannah. "Have a look through that while I find the valuation notices."

Her eyes flew down the two columns, her mortification growing at the red digits. *Dad! How could you let it get this bad?* "Uncle George, where is the cottage rental money listed?"

George ran a finger down a column before glancing at Dawn. "Hmm. Looks like I missed that. Dawn, are the tenants still happy? I mean, has the real estate agent said anything about them moving out?"

All eyes focused on Dawn and she bent her head forward, pressing spread fingers against her forehead as though willing the answer to reveal itself. Her shoulders slumped as she raised her eyes to meet George's. "Sorry, George. With John getting sick, I forgot all about that. They gave notice after Christmas and I meant to check with the agent about getting new tenants."

"So, the cottage is empty, Mum?" Hannah drew a deep breath while she waited for Dawn's confirmation.

"I suppose it is. I-I haven't followed it up." Her lip quivered, and Hannah hurried to her side, wrapping her arms around her.

"It's okay, Mum. We all understand, and no one is blaming you for anything. We just want to establish the facts so we know what we need to do." She smiled softly.

Jill and Susan continued to fuss over Dawn, and Hannah ached with love for her. In a few short weeks, her mother had aged. Black rings were visible under her eyes despite the layer of makeup, and her usually bright, smiling lips sagged at the corners.

For the next few minutes, Hannah shut out the muted conversation around her and concentrated on the sheaf of papers, scribbling furiously with the lead pencil she had grabbed from the jar in front of George. Tension pulled at the point between her eyes as she calculated. She dropped the pencil and stared at her mother.

Her heart squeezed while disbelief at her father's lack of financial management morphed into acceptance.

Dawn couldn't do this on her own. Hannah would save Fantail Ridge. She wouldn't leave her mother without a home.

CHAPTER 7

It was a social, more positive group that filled the dining room for breakfast the following morning, with everyone appearing refreshed after a good night's sleep. All except Hannah, that was.

"I've had a few ideas and am interested to hear what you all think," Hannah said.

While they sipped their coffee and tea, she pulled a piece of paper from her pocket, unfolded it, and smoothed out the creases with long, firm fingers. Hannah glanced around the waiting faces and gave a small nod.

"With what you provided us with last night, Uncle George, I have made some calculations and decisions on what I would like to do. Mum, you may or may not agree, but we need to start somewhere."

Dawn returned Hannah's smile from across the table, her hands clasped around the delicate bone china mug. "I'm sure you will have thought of all the answers, darling. Go on. We're listening."

"It seems they value the home farm a little higher than the run-off, but possibly only because it comprises four title deeds, whereas the run-off is one. The debt is higher than the valuation on either, but I believe that if we sell the run-off, and eighty percent of the cattle, we could service the balance of what we'd owe with the remaining cattle and sheep." She paused, glancing around the table to judge reactions. "Also, if we keep the home farm, we've got the added income of the cottage rental to help."

"But who will run the farm?" Tim asked.

Hannah took a deep breath before answering. "Me."

"But what about your job, Hannah? You love it so much and have studied hard to get where you are. I don't think your father really expected you to give it up." Dawn's face wore a worried look.

"Mum, Dad's not here anymore to help us. It is you and me, and no matter how much you do around the place, the bottom line is that you're not getting any younger."

Dawn pursed her lips, and Hannah grinned at her mother's raised eyebrows. "Sorry, Mum, but those are the facts—and we need to learn to work with them." She drew a deep breath before continuing. "Anyway, I've given my job a lot of thought and I will resign."

Surprised gasps resonated around the room. Dawn's jaw dropped.

"I've loved what I do, but I won't be losing any knowledge—just gaining opportunities to use those years of study in other ways."

Tim nodded his approval, and Susan smiled proudly at her, allowing Hannah's confidence to grow.

"Don't worry, Mum—and Uncle George. I'll talk to the bank before I send my resignation ... just to ensure they'll support us when we need it. At this time in my life, though, Fantail Ridge needs me—and I think I need it." She shrugged. "I can always get another job if things don't work quite as well as I hope they will."

The smile spread across her mother's face and Hannah let out a slow breath.

"There's nothing we can do about the past now, but there's plenty we can do about the future." Hannah spoke firmly, determined to involve her mother in her new plans and ideas. She knew Dawn would grieve her husband for a long time—as would she for her father. However, Hannah decided then and there that she would not allow Fantail Ridge to slip into the clutches of anyone else. It was theirs. Her beloved grandparents had toiled and struggled to turn the rough land into a profitable and beautiful farm, and, with the good fortune of prime meat and wool prices for much of her father's early reign, had also been the envy of the district. *It's a privilege for Mum and me to continue living there—and I WILL make it work.*

"Good on you, Han." Tim's beam widened while the

creases at the corners of his eyes rose to meet his hairline.

"Admirable, Hannah. If there's anything I can do to help you, you only have to ask." George nodded solemnly, his expression unchanging. Only those who knew him best, including Hannah, realised how pleased he was despite the seriousness he displayed.

Hannah took a sip of her tea, and for the first time since her father's funeral, it actually tasted warming and good. Around her, her family chatted about farming and happier times with John—ones she wanted to focus on too.

When she was finished her cup, she stood.

"Come on, Mum. It's time we headed home and started rethinking things."

Dawn gave a small nod and rose to her feet while Hannah gathered the cups and plates, letting her gaze drift around the room. As beautiful as George and Susan's home was, it was Fantail Ridge she wanted— and she couldn't wait to bring it back to a state of financial health.

———

THEIR JOURNEY BEGAN IN COMFORTABLE SILENCE UNTIL, minutes after they'd turned off the motorway and left suburbia kilometres behind them, Hannah glanced across at her mother.

"Mum, do you think when Dad apologised to us in the hospital, that the debt was what he meant?"

Dawn met her glance with wide eyes and fine lines forming on her forehead. "I thought he was apologising for leaving us both. Now that you mention it, perhaps he was referring to the mortgage." She shook her head. "I'm so sorry, Hannah. I didn't know things were this bad. You know your dad. He always looked on the bright side of everything and never liked to share his worries in case they upset us."

Fat lot of good that did in the long run.

"I'll miss the lupins." The random statement took Hannah by surprise, and she grinned at her mother.

"Mum, there're heaps of lupins in the garden at home now—and there are quite a few dotted through the plantations on Fantail Ridge, too, so it's not as though you'll never see one again."

"I know. But I helped plant those on the run-off the first year I lived here. They're very special to me."

Hannah's heart softened, and she reached out and rested her hand on her mother's. "I know, Mum. You did a great job, but now the grass has taken over so there aren't many left. Anyway, the government's decided they're a declared a pest in many areas, so I think it's best we contain them to the garden or places where we can control them—like the tree plantations."

"Really?"

"Yes, really. Don't worry. We can still grow them

anywhere that doesn't risk contamination of water-ways. Remember, I told you that when I was doing my degree?"

"Oh, I must have forgotten."

Hannah frowned. Was her mother's forgetfulness due to sorrow—or something worse? Dread coursed through her as she thought of Nanna Lil. Dawn's mother had developed dementia years before and had been in a secure aged-care unit, unable to remember or recognise anyone for years. Her difficult temperament had worsened and in the end, it had been a relief for everyone when she died.

Mild panic filled Hannah as she considered her mother's future. Chiding herself, she took slow, deep breaths, convinced it was grief in her mother's case, and nothing she need worry about.

Scruffy came bounding across the yard to greet them before Hannah had fully stopped. She slammed on the brakes and switched off the engine.

"You silly little boy. One of these days we won't see you in time." She chided and bent down to pick up the squirming bundle of wiry ginger and white hair. Hannah glanced over to the house paddock, relieved to see the three horses grazing and the other dogs waiting with pricked ears outside their kennels.

"Looks like the Bennetts have fulfilled their promise of taking care of the place. Everyone looks pretty content here, anyway."

"Give Scruffy to me, Hannah." Dawn reached out and took him from Hannah, burying her face in the dog's coat while his tail slapped frantically against her chest.

Hannah lugged the bags inside and unpacked before hastily stripping off her good clothes and pulling on jeans and a polo shirt.

She re-entered the kitchen as her mother took the final item from the box of groceries they had bought on their way through town.

"Why don't you put the kettle on, Mum, and make us a bit of lunch while I let the dogs off and check Delight's leg?"

"Okay, dear, will do." She closed the fridge door as Hannah shot her a smile and dashed outside.

———

As soon as Hannah had done a thorough check of the animals, she phoned Hugh and Andrew to thank them for their help and then sat down in her father's office to study the pile of mail before making a list.

Number one was to contact the solicitor and establish timeframes before major decisions could happen—like selling a part of the property. *There's no time like the present.* She dialled the number listed on the cover letter and waited.

Fifteen minutes later, Hannah placed the receiver

back in the holder and continued writing while the answers remained clear in her head. She detailed the plans to sell, amounts she thought the animals would go for—anything and everything related to the property, including unnecessary equipment.

"What did he say, dear?"

Engrossed in writing, Hannah jumped as her mother appeared by the desk.

"Well. The long and the short of it is that nothing happens quickly. It usually takes around six months before all the legal steps are complete, and only then can we actually list the run-off for sale."

Confusion clouded Dawn's eyes as she stared at Hannah. "Is that bad?"

Hannah shook her head and smiled reassuringly. "No, it's okay, Mum. While we wait for the legal stuff to be sorted out, we'll get the agent to find us another tenant for the cottage and get on with selling cattle. At least that should bring in enough money to satisfy the bank—for the moment, anyway."

Sighing contentedly, Dawn stroked Hannah's hair. "Good. I'm going out to the garden for a while. Is there anything you need me to do?"

"No. You go. I'll be fine. Don't bother bringing any flowers in for the vases though." She chuckled and glanced around the room. During the days between John's death and the funeral, the constant stream of visitors who'd called in had mostly also delivered a variety of either professionally arranged bouquets or bunches of flowers from their own gardens. The air in the room was heavy with the scent of lilies and roses.

Dawn sighed and disappeared through the kitchen door, with Scruffy following close behind.

The afternoon slipped away while Hannah phoned and emailed her way through the to-do list. At four o'clock, she reviewed her neatly outlined plans before closing her laptop and making her last call. Pulling the chair closer to the desk, she tapped her pen on the edge of the desk while she waited for her uncle to answer.

"Good afternoon."

"Hi, Uncle George. I'm ringing to let you know I've got the ball rolling on a few things." Hannah waited while he cleared his throat.

"Very good. Go on."

"Mum and I have an appointment with the bank early next week, so hopefully after that we'll know more about what they will or won't lend us, given the updated business plan."

"Business plan? You've done one already?"

Hannah grinned to herself. *I reckon you're loving being more involved again.*

"Well, not entirely. I guess it's more of a proposal that will hopefully satisfy the bank that we can meet our financial obligations—if we make the changes we've discussed." She twisted her ponytail around her fingers while she studied her notes.

There was a momentary silence at the end of the

phone before George spoke again. "Well done, Hannah. I'm impressed."

A surge of pride washed through her. Compliments from her aging uncle had always been rare, and when they came, were gold.

"So, what are your exact plans?" he asked.

"I'll email them through to you, Uncle George, but we'll get a tenant into the cottage and start sorting out cattle for sale to begin with. I've spoken to the stock agent, and he said he can come out on Friday to have a look at them. He'll help me select a truckload of weaner lambs to sell off in the next couple of weeks as well. By then, we'll have the bank's information and hopefully know what we can and can't afford to keep."

"Good, good." Hannah could hear the faint scratching of a hand against whiskers, and she grinned again.

"If we need money before we get paid for the cattle, I'll draw some out of my savings," she continued.

"You've done well, Hannah. Good girl. Ring me again after your appointment with the bank—and, of course, if there is anything else you would like to discuss."

"I will. Thanks, Uncle George."

She ended the call and stared at the list in front of her, chuckling. *He was a good boss.*

Stretching her back as she stood, Hannah stared at the pile of bank statements and payment reminders fluttering in the gentle breeze that blew through the window. "Okay, Uncle George. Here comes the email. As the family accountant, you need to know everything." She spoke out loud before opening a new message and attaching the document. *I wonder why Dad didn't heed your advice when he couldn't manage the debt?*

CHAPTER 8

"I appreciate you coming to see us, Hannah. And you, Dawn. Bob Sweeney's the name, branch manager." He shook both their hands and waved toward the short, brightly lit corridor. "Please, follow me."

As they trekked through the maze of partitions within the large, high-ceilinged room, Hannah breathed in the smell of polished timber and a hint of musty paper. Bob pushed open a door into a side office, then closed it firmly behind them. Showing them to a pair of bucket seats opposite, he positioned himself in a wide swivel chair, his middle-aged diminutive frame almost disappearing behind the desk. His black-framed glasses, the lenses thick and round, reminded Hannah of a photo from a WWII newspaper she'd found lining her grandfather's wardrobe when they'd moved into the homestead. A photo on the page depicting a politician had looked like a cartoon character to her, and embarrassment had filled her when her parents had laughed at her notion.

There was a moment of awkward silence and Hannah stifled a giggle. Why did things like this make her so nervous?

"How can we help you?" Bob clasped his tiny hands together and rested them on the leather desktop.

Hannah placed the pile of statements and correspondence in front of him. "As you know, things have been tough on the land lately, and now my father has passed away." She cleared her throat and Bob nodded.

"Very sorry to hear the sad news. Please accept my condolences."

Hannah returned his nod and Dawn smiled sadly.

"We are aware we can't sell the land until after the required legal steps are complete but have drawn up a plan to service the debt—for discussion and your approval," Hannah said.

Bob leaned forward and dragged his keyboard toward him before swiping a card along the side of the computer. The screen lit up, and Hannah gritted her teeth as the black and red digits appeared.

The following half hour ground slowly, with Bob poring over Hannah's plan and firing questions across the table. Hannah squirmed in her chair, crossing and uncrossing her legs, while Dawn stared through the window and picked at her fingernails.

After what seemed like forever, Bob drew himself up and smiled. "I believe we can still be of help to you both—provided the *powers that be* approve—and, of course, you pay the overdraft. I will draw up my recommendations and submit them to our loans department while, in the meantime, you implement your plan of selling stock as suggested."

Hannah's head spun with relief, and she touched her mother's hand gently. "So there's no problem selling cattle even though the farm isn't yet officially in our joint names?"

"Not that I can see. Your mother has been a part-owner for many years and therefore may continue operating as normal." He smiled again at both women, and Dawn clung to Hannah's hand.

"Thank you, Bob. That is a tremendous relief to us both, as you can imagine." Dawn clutched her handbag and stood before reaching over the desk to shake the man's hand.

"Pleasure. I'll be in touch as soon as I receive information from the loans department." He escorted Hannah and Dawn to the door and gave another nod, his balding head shining under the artificial light.

Hannah grinned at her mother as they stepped onto the pavement. "I reckon that deserves a celebratory morning tea at the Why Not café. What do you think?"

"Definitely." Dawn tucked her hand into Hannah's elbow as they marched down the hill.

While Hannah stirred her cappuccino, Dawn gazed through the window. Hannah touched her mother's hand.

"Penny for your thoughts?"

Dawn shook her head and shared a sad smile. "I was remembering the first time your father brought me here. It was not long after we moved and we'd had a row."

Hannah raised her eyebrows.

"We'd argued about him having lunch with his parents—as he had done his entire life. I expected him to come home. He was a bit shocked when I lost my temper." Dawn grimaced and Hannah giggled.

"I bet he was. I don't remember Dad ever raising his voice at anyone—not even the dogs."

"You're right. He didn't. I envied his calm temperament." She drained her cup and patted her mouth with the napkin. "Anyway, my tantrum worked. Every week after that, we came to town on a Friday, bought groceries and then came here for morning tea—and, he came home for lunch unless Granny invited us both to eat with them." She threw Hannah a rueful grin. "So what's next on the list."

"Sorting out the cottage for a new tenant?"

Dawn pushed her chair back and rose. "Right. Let's do it." She straightened her shoulders and linked arms with Hannah as they called goodbye to the waitress and headed outside.

———

HANNAH SAT BACK ON HER HEELS AND GAZED AT THE neat little house. "Were you happy living here, Mum?"

Dawn paused in front of the pile of weeds and leaned against the plum tree where the wide, circular bed had once bloomed with pansies and alyssum. Weeks of the cottage being empty had allowed spiders to make themselves at home. The area around each tree had been overlaid with matting, suppressing the worst of the weeds, however, when they'd arrived, the lawn resembled a hay paddock. Hannah and her mother had spent hours getting the place back in order—and now, it looked great.

"We were happy," Dawn answered softly, a wistful gaze on her face as she stared at the dwelling.

"Are you sorry we moved to the homestead?" A flash of concern furrowed Hannah's brow.

"No. Well, that is … it made sense to move when we did. Costs were rising and, as you know, we needed all the financial help we could get." She sighed and looked at Hannah, a smile playing around her lips. "If you get married, Hannah, you can have the homestead and I'll move back here."

Hannah snorted. "Huh. Presuming we can save the property first, it looks like we're stuck with each other for a good while yet then."

Dawn's smile widened. "Don't be like that. I'm just saying. I can't believe how much I hated this cottage when I first arrived." She grimaced. "I thought I was coming to a house like the homestead and was rather ungrateful."

Hannah glanced around the yard, taking in the mature trees, hedges, and remnants of what was once a beautiful and thriving garden. "Did you and Dad plant everything here?"

"Pretty much. With Granny's help most times." Dawn rolled her eyes. "I was hopeless—knew nothing." She gathered up the weeds and dumped them in the wheelbarrow. "Well, I reckon that's us done here. All we need now is a tenant who'll keep up the maintenance."

Hannah's stomach did a flip. A paying tenant was only one small element affecting the saving of Fantail Ridge.

That night before Hannah went to bed, she opened her laptop and began an email. It took less than a minute.

To Whom it may concern,

Please accept my resignation effective immediately.

Kind regards,

Hannah Simpson.

She inserted the human resources department with a copy to Brian, paused for a second—and hit send.

———

A BLOWFLY BUZZED AGAINST THE INSIDE OF THE LIVING room window, attracting Hannah's attention as she tipped her cup up and swallowed the cool water. April had arrived, bringing with it mixed weather patterns and cooler temperatures, but today was warm and still, a reminder that summer had not disappeared completely.

She opened the window and flicked the fly outside. "Get away, you pest." Then, dropping her gaze to her filthy shirt and jeans, she called to her mother.

"I'm going to have a quick shower."

"Okay," Dawn replied. "Mustering and drafting lambs has a way of demanding that."

Hannah grinned and wiped the sweat from her forehead, frowning at the blue dual-cab ute slowing outside the front gate. A rigid canopy with sliding windows covered the back tray, and a rust-coloured dog hung its head out of the near side. The four-wheel drive stopped, and she squinted. Who could that be? Hannah was familiar with most vehicles on the peninsula.

Her curiosity grew when a tall, dark-haired man stepped out of the vehicle, his hand resting on the dog's head as he looked around. She hurried outside, scraping the loose curls of hair from her face, and retying her ponytail. She slipped on her boots and paused next to her mother.

Dawn was on her knees, weeding the rose garden near the back door, and she struggled to her feet. "Who is it, Hannah?"

"Dunno, Mum. I don't recognise the vehicle. Has to be a stranger, though, to stop there."

Scruffy rushed past her, barking furiously as the man approached the rarely used entrance. Both neighbours and family ignored the old picket fence and pretty white gate, preferring to drive around the corner and into the vehicle entrance, entering the house yard via the side gate.

She took a step forward, then hesitated while Scruffy stopped in front of the man, wagging his tail and squirming with welcome. The man bent to pat the little dog, and Hannah walked toward him.

"Hello. Are you Mrs Simpson?" He held out his hand in greeting and Hannah blinked as she hesitantly reached to receive his handshake.

"Um. No, that's my mother. I'm Hannah."

She tilted her head back, her interest growing as deep chocolate-coloured eyes met hers. Both she and her mother were relatively tall, but under the visitor's gaze, Hannah felt small and a bit overwhelmed by his fit, muscly frame. "Can I help you?"

A confused look flashed across the man's handsome face. "Did the real estate agent ring you?"

"Not that I know of." Hannah frowned briefly. *Mum?* "Come and meet my mother. She may have taken the message." Hannah turned toward the house again, glancing sideways as the visitor's stride lengthened to match hers.

Dawn had remained beside the rose garden and as they approached, she inclined her head.

"Mum, did you receive a call from the real estate agent?" Hannah asked.

A look of guilt replaced the confusion flashing across Dawn's face. "Oh, yes. He called the other day to tell me someone was coming to look at the cottage." She turned to the man. "Is that you?"

Another wave of concern for her mother stabbed at Hannah. She faced their visitor. "I'm sorry about that. Would you like me to show you around?"

"I've already had a look." He fished in his pocket and pulled out a key. "The agent gave me this and told me to let myself in." He grinned sheepishly. "I've done that and rung to tell him I'll take it. Just thought it polite to come and introduce myself."

"Oh." Hannah couldn't think of anything to say. Her heart thumped, and she shot a glance at her mother. *This could be the end of our more immediate financial woes. A tenant—and a handsome one!*

Dawn had removed her gardening gloves and reached out to shake the man's hand. "And you are?"

"I'm sorry. How rude of me. The name's Justin, but everyone calls me Woody."

"Woody. Well, it's nice to meet you. When are you planning to move in?"

Hannah was grateful to her mother for keeping the visitor engaged while she gathered her wits.

"As soon as I can get the paperwork signed and

gather my belongings. Hopefully, by next weekend at the latest."

Dawn smiled at him while Hannah glanced down at her filthy shirt and grease-stained jeans.

"Do you work around here?" Embarrassed by her scruffy appearance, the words rushed out before Hannah could stop them.

He shot them a wide smile, displaying straight, white teeth and deepening the creases at the corners of his eyes.

"I'm a shearer but can turn a hand to most things." He shrugged. "I'd like to get a bit of work in the area— you know, fencing, mustering, shearing, crutching. Whatever's needed, really. I know my way around a cow shed, too, so I'm hoping some of the dairy farmers around here might need a holiday."

Great—I think? Hannah's thoughts ran amok. A strong pair of hands during busy times would be very welcome on the farm. However, the last thing she needed was a handsome distraction in her life. She had no desire to repeat history, and after her disaster with Todd, men were strictly off the agenda.

She straightened her spine and excused herself, headed back for the house. He might have been handsome and polite—but she wouldn't let a man distract her from saving Fantail Ridge.

CHAPTER 9

Poor Delight. Hannah's heart clenched as she dwelt on her beautiful mare. The wound had continued to heal well and Delight was enjoying being out in the paddock with Honeysuckle and Monty. However, her gait was stiff and uneven, and Hannah reluctantly accepted it would be many months before she could ride her again. While she stood in the middle of the field, studying the horse, she pulled her phone from her pocket and dialled Kevin.

"Gidday. How's my favourite mare?"

"Not good. She doesn't seem to be improving." Hannah bit back a groan.

"Don't panic Hannah. It's early days. Sometimes these types of injuries take a year or more. Give her more rest—and perhaps you could consider a side project?"

"Like what?"

"How would you feel about taking on another horse?"

"What do you mean? I'm here on the farm now. I don't need another show jumper?"

"I know. I've got a gelding here that needs a new home, and I thought he might be an excellent project for you."

"Okay. Tell me more," Hannah's heart pounded as she considered the possibility.

"I promised an elderly client I'd find him a suitable owner. He doesn't want anything for him—just someone kind who'll give him a chance."

"What's his story?"

"The horse has raced for a brief season, but he's too slow. You know what the racing industry's like. Thoroughbreds that don't make the grade are a dime a dozen. He's dead quiet to handle and doesn't seem to have any vices. Just needs work and a lifestyle that doesn't stress him too much, I reckon."

Hannah's stomach leapt as she'd weighed up the extra time she'd need to put into another horse. Add potential vet, and food bills. But a comfortable and suitable mount would make a huge difference to her workload. "What's his name?"

Kevin grunted. "They call him Slug. I think he's always been slow."

Hannah laughed. *Poor Slug. What a name. We'll have to change that.*

———

ON FRIDAY OF THE SAME WEEK, HANNAH HUMMED TO the music as she trundled south along the motorway, determined to keep her mind off the list of uncompleted farm jobs.

Buzzing with excitement at seeing Ellie again, she refused to think about the 'exit interview' that was waiting for her at the research station. They had not accepted her resignation lightly, and Brian had attempted to convince her that leave without pay would be a more secure decision—at least for the moment, anyway. However, Hannah had insisted. She would not allow the farm to fall into a neglected state and she certainly would not sell it to anyone else. There was no choice. *Don't worry, Fantail Ridge. I'm here for you.*

She pulled into the car park, scanning the area for a large enough spot to park the ute and horse float, and manoeuvred into a gap against the hedge at the far end. Slinging her bag over her shoulder, she walked the thirty metres before pausing and drawing a deep breath outside the front door. Entering the cool, brightly lit entry with its familiar smell of cheap antiseptic and coffee inspired a sense of déjà vu, and she glanced into the reception area. No sign of life. *Of course not. It's lunchtime.* Hannah grasped the timber handrail and hurried up the stairs, pausing outside the entry door to her old department.

"Hello!" Ellie rushed across the floor, throwing her arms around her as though it had been two years, not two months, since her friend had left. "Ooh, you've got so thin?"

Hannah pulled away from her stout, solidly built friend and grinned. "Hi to you too." Hannah glanced at her watch, smiling. "I'm a bit early, so I thought I'd clean out my desk before I see Brian and Karen. Then we can head to the café for lunch. What do you reckon?"

"Sounds great. Here, let me help you." She emptied the last of the photocopy paper and handed Hannah the empty box.

Hannah glanced at it with a tinge of regret. She'd never been a collector and disliked clutter, so there was little to show for her years of dedication to the company. A work diary, her delicate china teacup—it had somehow ensured the cheap black brew the company supplied tasted better than it looked—a few certificates confirming her work achievements over the years, and a handful of pens.

"That didn't take long, Ellie. Here, have a few more pens to add to your collection." Hannah chuckled as she handed them over. The remaining items barely covered the bottom of the box, and she raised her eyebrows. "That's it. Seven years' worth."

Ellie met her gaze with a grimace. "I miss you."

"Aww, you're a sweetie. I miss you too, but I have to do this. It's my heritage and my family and ... I suppose

I didn't realise how important it was to me until Dad died." She gave a gurgling cough as a lump formed in her throat. "We'll stay in touch. We can email. Maybe you could come and stay for a weekend sometime?"

"Ooh—I'd love to!"

Hannah glanced at the clock. "Hey, I'd better run now. See you soon."

"Okay. Looking forward to lunch." Ellie rubbed her stomach. "I'm starving."

Hannah laughed as she headed for the door. "You're always hungry."

———

"I'm so sorry, Hannah." Brian's long, thin face wore a hang-dog look, and Hannah choked back tears. *Damn it! I'd thought I was pleased to be out of all this.*

"I know. Thanks for your help." Hannah pushed her chair back and stood, plastering a firm smile on her face. "The family farm is important to me—more important than I realised, and I know I've made the right decision."

Both colleagues stood now, and Brian rested his hand on the door handle.

"Don't forget—if things don't work out as well as you hoped, we'll always be happy to have you back," Brian said.

Hannah smiled as she left the office. Her heart was light as she trod purposefully to collect her box of possessions and her friend. Disappointment still rankled at the loss of her long-hoped-for job, but in this moment, the realisation of how much she had been valued in her work was enough.

"Come on, girlfriend. Let's feed that skinny, starving body of yours." Ellie grabbed Hannah by the arm and they left the building, giggling like schoolgirls.

Two hours later, satiated by quiche and salad, an enormous piece of carrot cake and a cappuccino, Hannah sang as she drove to the Equine Centre.

The back of her vehicle was piled high with the last of her kitchen appliances and crockery, a suitcase containing linen, and the few items of clothing she'd left in the wardrobe. In the float, her lawnmower, and the remnants of horse feed from the shed filled one bay while the other remained empty except for a full hay net hanging from the D-bolt up front. The lease on the cottage would expire in less than three weeks, and, with the relevant paperwork now signed, the cottage clean and empty, and the keys handed back to the agent, Hannah looked forward to picking up her new horse.

Hope bubbled inside her. As Hannah rode around the arena, the horse pulled the reins through her hands and she gave him his head, relaxing into the saddle until he settled. Within seconds, he gave up all attempts at fighting and flicked his ears back and forth as though waiting for instruction. She walked the horse around the buildings, weaving in and out of hedged areas as she murmured to him. Finally, she deliberately urged him past a tattered horse rug casually thrown over a gate and flapping in the breeze. The gelding pricked up his ears, gave a snort, and trotted past without hesitation.

The resident pair of Dachshunds raced out from reception, barking furiously as Hannah approached. Watching with apparent interest, Slug barely batted an eyelid, stopping abruptly when Hannah drew rein. She slithered down his side as he dropped his head and nuzzled the dogs.

"They're old friends." Kevin stood outside the side door, drying his hands on a towel. "What do you think?"

"He's nice. I like him."

"So will you give him a chance?"

"Yep. I'll take him home and see how we go."

Slug was taller than Delight. His long, thin face, highlighted with a blob of white hair between his big coffee-coloured eyes, bent down and pressed gently against Hannah's stomach, his discussion with the dogs obviously over.

"You're a handsome boy, aren't you?" She rubbed him around the ears and ran her hands down his long legs, noting the sloping pasterns and strong hindquarters. *Should be good on the hills.*

After completing the paperwork, Hannah led the big-boned bay to the float. He clattered aboard without hesitation, his focus clearly on the full hay net.

"I told you he could be just what you need. Even if you only use him for a year or two while Delight gets back to normal, I reckon he'll be a handy fellow to have around." Kevin hoisted the tailgate up and latched it while Hannah closed the side door.

"He certainly seems promising. I guess we'll soon know." She shrugged and shot Kevin a grin. "I'm definitely not calling him Slug, though. To me, he feels like a Cruiser."

Kevin laughed. "Fair enough. Cruiser it is."

Hannah rested her elbow on the car door's open windowsill and crossed her fingers.

"Give me a ring at the end of next week and let me know how he's going," Kevin called.

She gave him a thumbs up and drove forward along the gravelled driveway before turning north toward her home.

———

It was late when she pulled into the Fantail Ridge yard. The sun had sunk behind the shadowy macrocarpa trees at the end of the house paddock, leaving a deep pink glow on the horizon.

"Red sky at night, shepherd's delight." Hannah grinned as she opened the door. A loud whinny resonated from the horse paddock, followed almost immediately by three heads popping over the gate. A nicker answered from the horse float. "We're home, mate. These larrikins are going to be your friends."

She unloaded Cruiser and tied him to the side of the float while she shifted Delight into the stable. Then, after transferring Monty and Honeysuckle into the adjacent paddock, she led Cruiser to the yard next to Delight and mixed them both a feed.

She patted Cruiser on the neck. "Plenty of time tomorrow for you to meet Monty and Honeysuckle."

Hannah pulled out her hair tie and ran her fingers through her thick locks. Tiredness she'd struggled to suppress for the last hour crept over her. Having left at four that morning, the hours of driving, socialising, and packing had consumed every thread of her energy.

"Hello, dear."

Hannah jumped as Dawn's voice penetrated the darkness. She turned to her mother's silhouette, a shadow in the already dark yard. "Hi, Mum. It's good to be home."

"You look shattered. Your dinner's in the oven and I've fed the animals, except the horses."

"Thanks, Mum. The horses are fine."

A warm glow flowed through Hannah as her mother linked arms with her and they turned toward the back door. The familiar gesture had been their tradition for as long as Hannah could remember. They supported each other physically as they negotiated rough ground and tough times.

———

Dawn pushed her empty plate aside and placed a cup of tea in front of them both.

"So tell me everything. How did you feel walking out of the research station knowing you don't work there anymore?"

Hannah swallowed the mouthful of chicken pie and delivered a detailed, step-by-step report of the day, including Brian's offer of a welcome back into their workplace, should she need it.

Dawn reached out and lay her hand over Hannah's. "I'm pleased about that, Hannah. I'd hate to think you feel you have no alternative to staying on Fantail Ridge."

Hannah smiled softly to hide her fierce determination. She was now committed to Fantail Ridge and, for as long as her mother was alive, would do everything in her power to keep both of them secure and comfortable on the farm. Her visit to the office had been the reminder she needed, reassuring her that her decision was the right one.

"I popped out to see Ed this morning," Dawn continued chatting while Hannah finished her meal, too tired now to invest energy in further conversation. "He was collecting and bottling the last of the honey before winter sets in. Said he'd love to see you when you've got time."

Hannah nodded and gave her mother a tired smile. "Did you tell him the latest news?"

"Of course. He seemed pleased to hear we'll be selling the run-off. Reckons the two farms would be too much for us, and he wants to talk to you about moving the bees onto Fantail Ridge."

Hannah's head shot up, and she stared at her mother, her exhaustion forgotten. "Really? I thought the Radley family were all lined up to buy him out, lock, stock, and barrel the minute he gave the word—bees included."

"Well ... no. I think your father's death has rattled him more than we realised. He's been putting his future wishes in writing—and giving away things that he says he no longer needs." Dawn jumped up and walked to the alcove in the living room corner where the office desk and filing cabinet competed with space for the sewing machine. "He gave me Hilde's sewing basket."

She held up a small handmade basket with a quilted lid. Hannah's heart leapt as she recognised the familiar container. Filled with threads, wool, and scraps, it was Bestemor's legacy—and held a lifetime of memories for Hannah. When she was small, she remembered the tall, quiet Norwegian woman allowing her to tip out the buttons from the little jar, spread them over the table and count them, matching colours and patterns. All the while, Hilde stitched patches on Ed's clothes, wove long strands of wool back and forth over the holes in socks, and sang Norwegian folksongs in her native tongue.

"I wonder if Ed thinks he's going to die soon?" Dawn spoke softly, and Hannah's heart leapt with compassion.

"Oh, Mum. He'll be a hundred years old in another month, so I'm sure it's probably crossed his mind. But we both know him well—he'll be wanting to get everything sorted out … just in case."

Dawn placed the sewing basket on the table and stared at it forlornly. "You're probably right. I guess all this death and sadness is raw for me at the moment."

Hannah stood and reached for her mother, hugging her tight. "Of course it is. Now sit down and watch telly while I deal with these dishes and have a shower."

Dawn obliged, and Hannah dumped the plates into the soapy water. Through the kitchen window, her gaze caught the silhouette of a possum running across the tank roof before leaping up into the nearby tree. Stars twinkled in the jet-black sky, and she drew a long breath. It was good to be home—even if it entailed a daunting amount of work.

Her head fizzed with excitement as plans formed. Tonight she would re-read the article about a new breed of sheep introduced into New Zealand, the White Dorper. She would email several breeders, requesting further information. Then tomorrow she would book the truck to pick up the last of the cattle for sale before taking Cruiser for an exploratory ride around the farm.

She gave a satisfied grin and pulled out the plug. She'd closed the door on her old life in Hamilton. Her new journey was just beginning.

CHAPTER 10

Hannah dropped the phone into its cradle and shot a worried glance toward her mother. "Did you know Barry had retired?"

Relaxed on the sofa, Dawn looked up from her sewing, her face blank. "Barry?"

"Yes, you know. The shearing contractor you've used for years."

"Oh, him. Um … I do vaguely remember your father mentioning he was getting out of it—probably around the time he started feeling unwell."

Hannah sighed and rubbed the back of her neck. "So, what are we supposed to do about getting shearers then?"

"I'm so sorry, darling. With all that's been happening here over the past few months, shearing had completely slipped my mind." Dawn bent her head again and snipped the thread with a pair of scissors.

"This is the last time I'm mending these jeans. I reckon it's time you bought some new clothes."

"I will—when I get time." The last thing Hannah wanted to share was how she'd blown half her annual clothing budget on a dress to wear at a work function of Todd's—a wasted expense. The function was to have been the week after she'd run from his house, vowing never to return. *Fat lot of good that was.*

"Why don't you give our new tenant a ring. Didn't he say he's a shearer?" Dawn tidied up the pile of mending, glanced at her watch, and rose to her feet. "I'll make us some lunch. It's my turn to check on Ed this afternoon."

Hannah propped her elbows on the desk and rested her chin in her hands as a vision of the bronze-skinned, dark-haired tenant flashed across her mind. "It's worth a try, I guess. Who are the other farmers around here using?"

Dawn paused for a moment and frowned. "I'm not really sure. Now you mention it, I think the few sheep farmers left in the area do their own shearing—or hire a single shearer rather than a team. So many have moved into deer or cattle."

Hannah stared at her mother, her concern growing. *Why does she keep forgetting these things?*

———

An hour later, Hannah braked outside the cottage gate. It had only been a few weeks since Justin moved in, but already, the place looked better than she remembered.

She stepped out of the vehicle and looked around as a red Kelpie raced toward her, its tail wagging furiously.

"Hello, little fellow. What's your name?" she asked, crouching down and stroking its coarse fur as it tried to lick her face.

"Red."

Hannah jumped, swinging her gaze as the deep voice resonated from beside the garage door.

"Oh. Hello. I didn't see you there." She turned back to the dog and stroked its head. "Of course—it's the colour of your coat. Why didn't I think of it?" She grinned at the dog's owner. "Woody, didn't you say?"

"You can call me Woody or Justin. I don't mind." His deep brown eyes sparkled and a grin spread across his face.

Hannah cleared her throat and nodded as heat crept up her neck. "Justin then."

Justin shifted his gaze from her to the dog. "Actually, I didn't name him because of his coat. Been living in Australia for a few years and worked at a station in the Pilbara for a while. There's a legend there of a red Kelpie dog who wandered the district for years. Everyone called him Red." He shrugged. "I was pretty impressed with the breed so I bought this fellow home with me … and of course, called him Red."

"Ah. Makes sense." Hannah rubbed her palms down the sides of her jeans, her pulse thumping in her ears. "Um. I want to ask you something."

"Okay. Fire ahead."

"Our shearing contractor has retired and because Dad has always dealt with that sort of stuff, I'm not sure what to do. We've always had our sheep shorn twice a year, in May and November … so I was wondering if you could help?"

"I'd be happy to. But first—do you mind me asking why twice a year?"

Hannah shrugged, her eyes widening. "It-it's something that's always happened here on Fantail Ridge. I suppose it's because we've always had Romneys and their fleeces get so long they would have been easier to manage if shorn twice—you know, less fly problems, easier joining and lambing."

"Yeah. Lots of fellas did that in the past—but that was when they got big money for the wool. You can still do it, but it'll probably cost you as much or more to have them all shorn than you'll get for the wool."

Hannah's pulse pumped faster as annoyance crept through her. *Why did Dad still do it then? Another unnecessary expense.* "So, are you suggesting that I only have the sheep shorn annually?"

Justin shook his head. "Not at all. It's totally your call. I'm just saying that with the reduced price of

Romney wool these days, and the increased shearing costs, it's not economical."

"Okay, so … if you were in my position of trying to manage the stock as well as I can on a tight budget, what would you do?" she asked, resisting the temptation to tap her foot.

"I'd crutch them now, before winter, instead of shearing. That'll cut your costs right down—and make the job a lot quicker. Leave taking the wool off them until later in the year."

Hannah chewed her lip while she absorbed the suggestion. Should she make such a drastic change? It made sense. She drew a slow breath. "Thanks. Um, how are you placed to give me a hand with crutching?"

"Happy to. Got a job drafting calves and drenching sheep out near the Heads for a couple of days later this week, but we could make a start next week if that suits?"

"Great, thanks." Hannah's insides did a somersault as she met his grin. "I'll start bringing them in over the weekend. I had to clean up some of them more than a month ago, but there's still about two thousand."

"Goodo. We'll get them crutched within in a few days. I charge the standard rate and will invoice you once the job's done. Does that suit?"

"Oh, yes, of course. Thanks." Hannah squirmed under Justin's gaze. *I'm supposed to be an efficient businesswoman. How embarrassing.*

Justin walked beside her as Hannah returned to her ute, her nerves jangling with anticipation.

"See you on Monday morning then?" she asked.

"Yep. I'll be there around seven. Get my combs sharpened and will be ready to start at seven thirty."

She bent to pat the dog again before climbing into the driver's seat. "See ya Monday," she called, and she drove away, careful not to look in the rear-view mirror.

———

THE FOLLOWING FEW DAYS FLEW AS HANNAH DEVELOPED a pattern of spending half an hour with Delight before riding Cruiser around the farm to check fences, water troughs, and any problems with the stock. Her mother dealt with the routine of feeding the chooks, cat, and the bulk of the housework, and Hannah's relief was palpable.

Hannah ached for her mother. The quiet sadness, coupled with long periods of her staring through the window, increased Hannah's pain. Her own grief was hard enough to deal with—and she could only imagine the depth of her mother's after living with the love of her life for forty years.

Lengthening her stirrups, Hannah prepared for Cruiser to misbehave and she talked soothingly to him as they rode behind the mob of sheep. "Good boy. We'll get this lot closer to the shed and then we'll go back and bring another flock in. That should give you the hint, shouldn't it?"

The horse flicked his ears and snorted as he picked his way across the culvert in the gully. Afraid that Jet's big bark might frighten the horse, Hannah had left him at the kennel, allowing Lass, the quieter Border Collie, to weave silently back and forth, her focus varying only between her mistress and the sea of cream-coloured bodies in front of her.

The big gelding settled quickly, his stride firm and purposeful, and Hannah relaxed. "I think you're enjoying this new life."

By Monday, Hannah had the first thousand sheep packed into the shed and yards outside while the balance filled the paddocks close by. She and Dawn had risen before daylight, completed their daily chores, and prepared thermos flasks and an icebox full of food.

"Are you sure you'll be alright outside, Mum?" Hannah asked as Dawn pulled her gloves on and tramped down the ramp to the swirling flock of sheep where the golden morning sun cast shadows in the yards.

"Of course, darling. I've been doing this job since you went away to university, don't forget—and I'm not ready to give it up yet." Dawn laughed. "You worry about what goes on inside the shed, and I'll take care of the outside."

Justin had arrived as Hannah was pushing more

sheep into the catching pens, and he gave a wave before switching on the grinder and sharpening his combs. She grinned. *At least you know your way around a woolshed.*

"I'm ready when you are." He leaned over the pen door as Hannah shoved her hair into a bun on the top of her head.

"Good. Thanks. I'll take the stand next to you and do my best. Mum said she'll keep the sheep up to us and will count them out afterwards, but she'll need help from time to time."

"Of course. Don't push yourself. I'll get into the swing of things and keep going. We should get them all done in five days, I reckon." He smiled at her and squeezed oil onto the handpiece. "Let's get into it."

Pleased she had crutched the fly-affected sheep a month and a half before, Hannah worked methodically, finding her rhythm after the first few and deciding not to even attempt to keep up with Justin. His hands flew —deftly turning each sheep and shearing around their eyes before bending lower and removing the wool from the tail area in seconds.

He was determined, a fierce worker, but his voice was kind as he spoke to the sheep, getting the job done —there was something special about that combination in a shearer. It wasn't always something Hannah had seen in her parents' farmhands.

At nine thirty, Dawn appeared in front of the two of them and pointed to the mugs of hot tea and a plate of sandwiches and fruit cake. Dawn cupped her hands around her mouth and yelled, "Smoko time!"

Hannah gratefully stretched and strolled to the basin to wash her hands. Returning to the makeshift table, she picked up a mug of tea and plonked herself on the shed floor, her back pressed against the wooden slatted wall. Her eyes followed Justin as he pushed the sheep down the chute and moved to the corner, lathering his hands, arms, and face with soap before rinsing and reaching for the towel.

"Thanks, Mum. How're things going outside?"

Dawn picked up a mug of tea and grinned.

"All good. Don't worry about me. As long as this weather holds, we'll keep going until we've got the job done." Dawn passed the container of sandwiches to Justin as he lowered himself to the floor. "Tell me, Justin, where on earth did the name Woody come from? Were you an arborist?"

Justin chuckled. "No. That's my name. Justin Woods."

Dawn's mouth dropped open and her hand froze in mid-air, her sandwich poised. "Justin Woods. Son of Carol?"

Justin raised his eyebrows and chewed silently.

Who was Carol? And why do you seem alarmed Mum? Her appetite forgotten, Hannah studied the two of them, waiting for Justin to answer.

"Yep. Carol is my mother. She left South Head after

my father died. Did you know her?" He paused, staring solemnly at Dawn.

"Y-yes. We were friends, sort of. Kept in touch for a few years and then nothing. They returned my Christmas card, marked it as 'unknown at this address', and neither Ed nor I heard from her again."

"Hmm. That'd be right. I was only a little fella—about five, I think, because I'd just started school. Anyway, Mum's parents had both died by then, and she met and married Nigel." He almost spat the name, and Hannah blanched.

"You didn't get on?" Dawn probed quietly, as though half expecting a rebuttal.

"Not really. He wasn't cruel or violent. Just controlling. He made Mum produce every grocery docket and begrudged her meeting anyone for lunch or a cuppa. He wouldn't let her go to work anymore so she could be at his beck and call. They didn't have kids, so it was just me—piggy in the middle." He reached for another sandwich and sat back, studying the leafy green rocket leaves spilling from its interior. He took a huge bite and chewing slowly, continued speaking, pausing only to swallow. "I left when I was fifteen. Lucky, really. I was pretty rebellious, so I suppose I could've got into real trouble. A mate of our neighbours' was looking for a new shed hand for his shearing gang, and he took me under his wing. I lived with the contractor's family after that and never went back."

"Is she … is she alright? Your mother, I mean," Dawn said.

"Yeah. She's fine. The old fella had a heart attack while I was in Australia. That's why I came home. Helped her get settled into a nice little house in Hamilton, and now she works part-time in a dress shop." He shrugged. "Happy as a pig in mud, apparently."

"Oh, that is good to hear. I'm sorry she had such a bad time though." Dawn shot him a sympathetic smile.

"Yeah. Me too. I don't know how so many women seem to end up with the same type of men that ruined their lives the first time 'round. From what I've heard, she got a rough deal with my father too."

Hannah's eyes widened. *How come Mum kept this local gossip from me?* She glanced at her mother, shocked at the soft, knowing smile that touched her lips.

"So, what brought you to South Head? A need to see where your life began?" Dawn ignored Hannah's questioning gaze as she continued the conversation with Justin.

"That's it. Mum always raved about what a nice place it was to live—she just didn't like the life she had with my father. So I thought I'd poke up here for a few months and have a look."

"And here you are," Hannah said.

Justin swivelled his gaze to her and smiled, his teeth gleaming against his tanned face. "Yes. And here I am."

And Hannah couldn't help but be very pleased he was.

CHAPTER 11

Clean, white sheep filled the yards, indignant bleats filling the air as they waited to be released. Hannah rinsed out the drench gun and hung it on the hook inside the loading dock, warm with gratitude. Without Justin's help, she and her mother would have been drenching the freshly shorn sheep until well after dark —or worse still, would have had to bring them all back in again the following day for their routine medicine. She turned to meet Justin's smile as he zipped up his gear bag.

"Thanks heaps, Justin. Good timing I reckon." Hannah pointed to the dark bank of clouds building in the western sky. "I'd better get this lot back to the paddock before that gets any closer."

"No worries. Call me if you need a hand with anything else."

Dawn hurried across the yard, pulling her work

gloves off as she walked. "Don't head off yet, Justin. I want to ask you something."

Both he and Hannah turned to face Dawn as she drew close, a hand on her breastbone as if she were out of breath.

"Sure. What is it?" Justin said.

"We have an elderly friend here on the peninsula. He lives about ten kilometres farther out—close to where your parents' farm was, actually. Anyway, it's his hundredth birthday this weekend, and the community is having a get together for him on Saturday afternoon. I was wondering if you'd like to come?"

Justin's eyebrows rose, and he shrugged. "If you think I'd be welcome, sure? Did my parents know this fellow?"

"Your mother did. She and I used to help him with the animals regularly. He rescued injured wildlife and was a skilled teacher. I think he enjoyed having visitors as he never married and had no children of his own."

Justin gave a soft grunt. "Sounds interesting."

"I think he'd like to meet you. He and his sister— now deceased—kept in touch with your mother more than I did. I think it quite upset them when the letters stopped coming. It would be nice for him to know why —and to know you are living here now," Dawn gabbled on. "Hannah will collect him about two o'clock, so we hope everyone will be at the hall waiting by half past two. It's not a surprise—he didn't want that." She drew a breath.

Hannah grinned, unable to take her eyes off the handsome figure against the setting sun. "You wouldn't dare refuse after all that, would you?"

Justin smiled widely. "I certainly wouldn't. I'll be there."

Dawn lay her arm over Hannah's shoulders as Justin's ute drove away. "What do you think of him? The two of you seemed to work well together. Any sparks?"

Hannah looked at her mother, shaking her head while her insides fluttered uncontrollably. "Mum! Stop trying to play matchmaker."

Dawn lifted her chin and laughed for the first time since John had died. Hannah smiled at her, delighted to hear the longed for sound.

"Well, you haven't dated since Todd. And I know there's been a lot going on, but that's no reason not to have a little fun. And Justin? He looks like he could be fun."

Don't be ridiculous. "No, Mum. He's a nice guy but you know as well as I do, the last thing I need in my life right now is another boyfriend. The scars haven't even faded after the Todd disaster." She turned away, walked toward the horse yard when she halted. "Justin said his mother had a tough time with his father. Do you know in what way?"

Dawn frowned. "He was a nasty piece of work. Violent and, from what I understand, an alcoholic. After he died, I heard he'd been like that for years. To this day, I could never understand what Carol saw in him." She shrugged. "Times were different then. Living with our partners before marriage was frowned upon, and even dating was so much harder than it is now. I suppose Carol fell in love with him—and didn't realise what he was really like until it was too late."

Hannah shuddered. "Poor Carol. Sounds as though she had a lucky escape." She'd heard domestic violence and alcoholism sometimes recurred in subsequent generations. Would Justin follow in his father's footsteps?

Uneasiness crawled through her. He seemed so nice. Could it be a front?

All the more reason to keep her heart to herself and not get sucked in by good looks and capability.

"Bye, darling. See you later." Dawn's call jolted Hannah out of her reverie, and she waved.

"See you soon, Mum." Then she continued toward Cruiser. *Yep—he's a pretty useful employee, though.*

Slipping her foot into the stirrup, she threw her leg over the saddle and turned the horse toward the flock of sheep grazing at the end of the paddock. "Here, Lass!"

The little Border Collie flew over the railing and wove her way across the grass, circling the flock in a black and white flash. As the sheep swirled in a thick cluster, Hannah urged Cruiser into a canter, trailing them as they surged down the slope. She rode wide, reaching the gate at the bottom of the hill ahead of the sheep while Lass controlled the mob. She bent to open the gate, throwing it open before steering the gelding away and letting the mass flow through the gap into the fresh paddock. Glancing back at the woolshed, her chest tightened at the sight of Dawn trudging toward the homestead, her bright pink cap bobbing. *Poor Mum. You're so tired. I couldn't have done it without you today.*

Almost immediately, she imagined her mother's retort. *"I've got plenty of years left in me yet, my girl!"* Hannah chuckled. She may not have a man, but she didn't need one. With a mother like Dawn, she had all the love she needed.

———

"ARE YOU SURE YOU'RE ALRIGHT, BESTEFAR?" HANNAH tucked the old man's walking stick behind the passenger seat and paused.

"Of course I am." Ed patted his breast pocket. "I've got my speech, my glasses so I can read it, and I'm being waited on by the most special young woman in my life. What more do I need?"

"Righto." Hannah smiled and closed the door carefully.

Twenty minutes later, she parked directly in front of the hall porch entry, the revered space kept for the guest of honour on local occasions such as this. Dawn was waiting on the bottom step and a crowd of neighbours flanked the car park.

"Oh, my goodness. I didn't expect this many people."

Hannah had to lean over to hear the old man's mumbled words. She patted his hand. "You're a special person. I don't think anyone else in the district has made it to their hundredth birthday—especially one who's lived here for most of it."

Dawn wrenched open the passenger door and bent down so her face was level with Ed's. "Are you ready to face the crowd?"

He held his hand out to her, and she steadied his frail body as he struggled out of the vehicle. A wide smile spread across his wrinkled face as Hannah handed him the walking stick. "I certainly am. Let's begin."

Progress into the hall was slow. The crowd swelled —a mix of local farmers and their families, past members of the community, and a handful of new residents—all eager to wish Ed well and shake the hand of the legendary Norwegian. As Ed's pace slowed, Hannah guided him to a chair at the front of the hall while Hugh Bennett tapped on the microphone. It screeched and crackled before his voice boomed through the building.

"Good afternoon, everyone. Thank you for coming." Hugh stopped and adjusted the volume on the speaker before continuing. "This is a special occasion—one we have not had the pleasure of experiencing before and, on Ed Hansen's behalf, I would like to welcome you here today to help him celebrate this incredible mile-stone." He turned to Ed and smiled. "Before we enjoy the delicious afternoon tea that is waiting, Ed would like to say a few words."

He stepped back and Dawn and Hannah each took an arm and helped Ed to his feet. As she stood in front of the sea of familiar faces, a warmth flooded through Hannah's veins and a strong sense of belonging gripped her. *This is my community. People I have grown up knowing and neighbours I will never forget. I can imagine how Ed must feel.*

At the back of the hall, a tall, dark head appeared between Charlie and Bev, Fantail Ridge's immediate neighbours, and butterflies fluttered inside her. She plastered a smile on her face and tore her gaze from Justin to the stooped frame of the elderly gentlemen beside her.

Chairs scraped and the buzz of conversation stilled as guests sat down or leaned against the wall.

Ed grasped Hannah's hand as she turned to walk away, and she looked back at him with surprise. "Stay here with me, Hannah, and you too, Dawn. Please?"

"Of course we'll stay with you." Dawn took a step forward, urging Ed to move closer to the microphone while Hannah fidgeted with one of her earrings.

"A-hem." Ed cleared his throat and swung his gaze between Dawn and Hannah. His above-average height had diminished over the years, and now he barely stood two centimetres taller than either woman. He took out his reading glasses and pushed them onto his face before extracting a folded piece of paper from his pocket. Clearing his throat again, he began speaking, his voice soft and a little shaky. You could have heard a pin drop as he began.

"Thank you all for coming today. Most of you know me well and have probably heard a little about how I came to live at South Head. However, I would like to share some of my story and offer my heartfelt thanks to all of you who have made the past eighty-five years a life worth living." He rustled the paper and straightened his shoulders before continuing. "In 1921, I was shipwrecked on the west coast of this peninsula, a fifteen-year-old boy from Trondheim, Norway. For many years, I had no memory, so I hid, believing myself to be a stowaway or an escaped prisoner."

A gasp sounded from somewhere in the crowd.

"I survived, thanks to the storekeeper down at the old Waioneke wharf—long gone now—who allowed me to help him in exchange for food and necessities. During those years, the Simpson and Bennett families showed me kindness and friendship, but it wasn't until I had an accident several years later that my memory returned and I realised how truly special these people were. Of course, that generation is no longer here to celebrate with us, but today I am lucky to have Dawn and Hannah Simpson with me—and of course, two generations of the Bennett family. I am proud to be a New Zealander, to have fought in the war for this beautiful country, and to have enjoyed a healthy and happy life on this peninsula."

He stopped, his chest heaving, and Hannah shot her mother an anxious glance. Both women stepped a little closer to him.

"Thank you to all those who helped my sister, Hilde, adjust to life here," he continued and Hannah raised one eyebrow, a little surprised. "Even though her time was short, it was precious to us both. Norway will always be dear to me, the country where I grew up, but today, I am fortunate to share my birthday, my thanks, and my appreciation with you all."

Exhausted, Ed's knees began to buckle and both Hannah and Dawn leapt forward and grabbed him, before stepping back and lowering him into the chair.

He coughed and waved an envelope, his voice rasping and faint. "My letter from the Queen."

Clapping filled the air as everyone stood up. Someone toward the back broke out in song, and those around him joined in the rendition of "For He's a Jolly Good Fellow." As voices quietened, two men emerged from the depths of the kitchen, carrying a gigantic birthday cake.

It was almost an hour later before Hannah could leave Ed to the throng of well-wishers and help herself to a plate of food. She'd just taken a large bite of scone, slathered with strawberry jam and cream, when a man's voice startled her.

"Hmm. Look at all this food. The locals certainly know the way to a man's heart."

Hannah whipped around at Justin's familiar tone and met his grin. She swallowed her mouthful, and a dry crumb caught in the back of her throat. She gagged, heat rising on her neck as she coughed repeatedly. Grabbing a paper napkin from the table, she pressed it against her mouth and turned away. Tears filled her eyes.

"Whoa. Don't choke to death on me!" His eyes filled with concern. "I'll get you a drink."

Her gaze followed his slim, athletic frame dressed in jeans, a pale blue shirt, and a leather jacket. *Jeepers, you're handsome. Shame you could be dangerous—not that I can afford any distraction even if I was interested..*

He returned a second later, holding out a glass, and she took it, her cheeks burning as she tried to regain her composure.

"Sorry about that. I didn't mean to give you a fright," he said.

She shook her head and attempted a smile. "Do you always sneak up on people like that?"

"Of course not. Let's get a bit of fresh air." He grasped her elbow and guided her out the kitchen door and down the steps beside the water tank. He pointed to the remaining food on her plate. "This looks like a nice place to sit and eat without choking." He plonked himself on the top step. Hannah lowered herself down beside him. "Beautiful food isn't it." He patted his stomach. "I've eaten more than my fair share."

"Have you talked to Ed?" Hannah threw the remnants on her plate to the birds and wiped her sticky fingers on the napkin.

"Yes. Not for long, but he's asked me to visit him tomorrow. I said I'd give him a hand with firewood or anything else he needs."

Hannah gave a brief nod. "That's great. He doesn't chop his wood anymore—his neighbour across the road does it for him, but I'm sure he'd be happy to have you around anyway. There's always something to do."

Reluctantly, she stood and faced him, wishing the afternoon would last forever. He caught her hand.

"Don't go yet—please?"

She met his pleading eyes, like melting chocolate and collapsed on the step beside him. "I should be helping in the kitchen."

He glanced over his shoulder where a team of women were talking and laughing as they washed dishes. "Looks to me like they've got more than enough helpers." He grasped her hand and pulled herself to her feet. "Come on, let's go and find a nicer place to sit and talk."

His hand felt warm and dry and Hannah's heart pounded. As they rounded the corner near the parked cars, Charlie's booming voice followed them.

"Hey Justin. Give us a hand with these chairs, would you?"

They stopped and gazed at each other. Hannah chuckled ruefully.

"You're part of the community now."

Justin shrugged, his grin widening. "Looks like I'll have to postpone our chat until another time."

She nodded. "Okay, catch you later." And she walked back inside, confused. *How could a man I barely know turn me into such a blithering idiot?*

CHAPTER 12

Hannah helped an exhausted Ed out of the car, then waited while he leaned on his walking stick and appeared to survey his home and garden.

"We'd better get those beehives moved to Fantail Ridge soon, Hannah," he said.

She followed his gaze to the four towers of hives tucked amongst the shrubs and flowers. "They look heavy."

"Oh yes, they will be. We'll need some help, but with the cold weather coming, it will be a perfect time to move them and let them settle before spring comes. I'll have a word with young Justin tomorrow and see if he'd mind giving us a hand."

Hannah's heart lurched. "You can't lift them, and I think we'll need more than one man." She didn't need to be in Justin's company—quite the opposite.

"Hannah. Are you listening?"

She started as Ed's voice penetrated her thoughts. "Sorry, Ed. I was miles away. What did you say?"

"I said—I'll arrange the helpers if you could bring the truck to transport the hives on. Probably in another two or three weeks."

"Of course. Come on now. Let's get you inside and light the fire."

Half an hour later, Ed shuffled his chair close to the crackling flames before Hannah lay a blanket over his legs and placed a tray with soup and toast on his lap.

"Mrs Anderson said she'd pop in about eight o'clock and see how you're getting on." Hannah frowned, wondering if she should call in at the Anderson farm on her way home and ask her to come earlier. It had been a big day for the old man, and he looked done in.

"Don't you worry about me, Han. I'll watch a bit of television and sleep well. Thank you again for the party." He held his hand out and Hannah took it before bending down to plant a kiss on his cheek.

"Righto. Mum will be out to see you tomorrow. I'm going to be doing a bit of research on White Dorpers."

Ed sparked up immediately, his grey, bushy eyebrows lifting. "White Dorpers?"

"Yes. I've been reading excellent reports about them and thought that with the need to diversify to make ends meet, it might be worth buying a couple of rams and putting them with a small flock of our older ewes. Apparently they're incredibly tough, and I thought they might strengthen the prime lamb side of our business."

Ed stared at her for a moment without speaking. "You're the right person for that farm, Hannah. You've always been a thinker."

A warm glow filled Hannah, and she hugged him gently. "Thanks, Bestefar. So you agree I need to diversify?"

"I do. Not just with the sheep. Consider other options too. There are plenty of ways to improve the land and fulfill a need—not just for you, but for the future and the people of New Zealand. Make your mother as proud of you as I am." He paused and shared a gentle smile with her. "It would delight your Grandmother Alice to see what a wonderful young woman you've become."

She nodded as tears welled in her eyes and let his words seep into her soul.

———

THE FOLLOWING MORNING, HANNAH WAVED GOODBYE to her mother as dark clouds built on the horizon. Settled in the office, Hannah glanced through the window and switched the light on. By eleven o'clock, rain slashed the panes and ran noisily along the guttering. She picked up the phone and walked to the armchair in the centre of the living room, where the drumming on the roof had lessened.

"Hello? I am phoning about the rams you have

advertised for sale," she said and settled into the comfy chair next to her notebook and pen.

Scribbling furiously, Hannah jotted down notes and ticked off the list of questions she had planned to ask the breeder. Her excitement grew and by the end of the call, she sat back, her heart thumping harder.

She glanced down at Scruffy, half asleep on her feet. "Oh, my God. I've just ordered two ridiculously expensive White Dorper rams. Thank goodness I still have some of my savings." The little dog opened one eye and then closed it again. Hannah chuckled. "A cup of tea is in order, I think. Move old fellow."

She poured herself a hot drink and returned to the office, her pulse racing as she studied the figures she had written.

The phone rang, and she jumped, splashing tea on the desk.

"Hello?" She leaned over the spill and wiped it off with the sleeve of her shirt.

"Hello. Is that Mrs Simpson?" The male's voice was unfamiliar, confident, and loud.

"No, it's Hannah, her daughter. Can I help you?"

"Good. Name's Trevor. I'm the new rural real estate agent for the area. I believe you've got a farm for sale."

Hannah blanched. It was not a secret. The bank manager, several local farmers, and even the company that managed the rental cottage were aware the run-off would be for sale—in time. It was the wait for the legal period of estate management to be fulfilled that was holding things up. So who is this guy? And how did he know about it?

"Um. Well, not yet. My father only passed away a couple of months ago, so I'm afraid it won't be able to go on the market for a while yet."

"I understand." An impatient tone filtered into his voice, and Hannah's hackles rose. "I have a buyer lined up for you."

"But we haven't even decided on a sale price?"

"You don't need to. My buyer's offer is fair and realistic, based on land sales in the area. He wants that block of land and will meet the market to achieve it."

Hannah's stomach flipped. Annoyance filled her, and she snapped back, "I'm very sorry, but I can't consider anything at this stage. You can contact our lawyer if you wish. He will advise when it's likely to be available for sale. Thank you for calling. Goodbye." She hit the 'end' button and replaced the handpiece in the cradle. "Cheek of the man!"

The rain continued to lash down as her mother's car pulled into the yard. Shoving her feet into gumboots and throwing an oilskin coat around her shoulders, Hannah grabbed an umbrella and rushed out to meet Dawn.

"That was a slow trip home. The rain pelted down the entire way, and I had trouble keeping the car on the road in places. It was frighteningly slippery." Dawn slammed the door and huddled under the brolly as they rushed into the boot room.

"How was Ed this morning?" Hannah asked, shaking the droplets off the umbrella.

"He's a little tired—to be expected after talking to so many people yesterday. But he really enjoyed his afternoon and is looking forward to Justin coming to see him later." Dawn kicked off her wet boots and slid her feet into slippers. "How was your morning? Did you get hold of the people about the rams?"

"I did." Hannah grinned and clenched her fingers together. "I've bought them!"

Dawn shot her a surprised look. "That was quick. I thought you wanted to see them first?"

"I did. They emailed me the photos and information while we were talking and said they didn't list these two because they thought they were a bit young. But after printing the catalogue, they regretted not including them." She shrugged. "I decided that the expense and time required to look at them was better invested in the actual animals."

"Good point," Dawn said.

"The guy was very nice. He said if I paid the reserve for them, they'd add them to the after-sale delivery run they've got planned for next week. So … they should land here a few days after that."

"Oh, that's exciting."

Dawn headed for the door into the passage, and Hannah called after her. "Oh, a bloke rang about the farm sale too."

Dawn stopped and inclined her head, frowning. "Really? It's not for sale yet though, is it?"

Hannah gaped. Had her mother seriously forgotten? "Of course it's not. I told him that. Someone must have spread the news, because he seemed to know all about it and has a buyer—apparently."

"Pfft. Those agents are always full of rubbish. I'll give the lawyer a call this afternoon and let him know anyway in case he needs to investigate the offer—or the so-called agent."

While she filled the bread pockets and placed them on the sandwich toaster, Hannah contemplated the agent's call. On one hand, it would be good to know the sale would be quick and clean, but on the other, the brash manner of the man and the concept of the family land actually leaving their control was daunting. A thread of unease rattled her—not only about the land sale. It was time to convince Dawn it was time for a health check.

———

"THERE'S NOTHING WRONG WITH ME!" DAWN SNAPPED. Hannah scooped up the last fork full of risotto before her mother reached for her empty plate.

"There probably isn't, Mum. But you've had a very stressful year and you've taken great care of Dad. Now it's time to look after yourself—and the first thing we need to consider before we launch into managing this farm on our own is that you're in good health." Hannah dropped her shoulders, her eyebrows raised.

Dawn shook her head in silence before stomping into the kitchen.

Hannah grinned to herself as she heard the kettle switch on. *A cuppa solves everything.*

It obviously worked, as the following morning as Hannah returned to the kitchen after the morning round of feeds, she heard the click of the phone being replaced.

"You'll be pleased to know I have an appointment with the doctor first thing on Thursday. The receptionist has noted it's for a full check-over."

Hannah nodded. "Thanks, Mum. I'm sure everything will be fine—better to be sure than sorry though. I'll make the toast while you do the tea."

While Hannah spread butter on her toast, she glanced into the mug her mother passed her. Black tea. Hannah blinked. She had never drunk black tea—the milk was as important as the leaves—and had always been the case for both her and her parents. *Oh Mum, I'm really pleased you're seeing the doctor soon.*

———

THE RAIN CONTINUED FOR DAYS AS WINTER SET IN, AND it took Hannah some convincing to get Dawn to drive to town for her doctor's appointment.

As she glanced at the pile of muddied clothes

mounting up on the wash house floor, Hannah sighed. She waved goodbye to her mother and strode to the stables to feed Delight. The mare had been locked up for days to avoid her slipping and damaging her leg in the mud. Her patience appeared to be wearing as thin as Hannah's.

Frustration built as Hannah worried about her mother while steering the tractor and hay trailer across the farm to feed the stock. The heavy, deeply treaded wheels dug into the tracks and slipped dangerously close to the edges. *God, this is a nightmare!*

Hannah turned to Lass. Pressing her smelly, wet-dog body against Hannah, the collie perched on the tiny platform next to the tractor seat.

"These tracks should've been re-gravelled over summer. Poor Dad. So much to do and unable to achieve anything because he was too stubborn to admit he was sick."

Lass flapped her hairy tail, flicking more mud over them both. Hannah gave a small laugh and patted the dog.

When she returned to the homestead, it shocked Hannah to discover the house empty except for Raga-muffin and Scruffy, fast asleep on the couch. She peered through the rain.

"Mum should have been home hours ago!" She picked up the cat and held him against her, his warm, heavy body slumping against her. "No point calling her mobile phone. Even if it is switched on—which is unlikely–the service is poor and patchy and I don't want her pulling over to answer it and getting bogged on the roadside." Scruffy looked at her, sneezed and rolled onto his back, his feet stuck in the air.

When the sound of a car engine speeding up the hill eventually penetrated the quiet house, Hannah threw her coat over her shoulders and rushed out. Weak with relief, Hannah stumbled as she reached the gate. Steadying herself against the solid timber, she unlatched it and strode toward the car.

Snatching the driver's door handle, Hannah hauled it open. "Where have you been? It's been dark for ages. I thought you must have had an accident or something!"

Dawn struggled wearily out of the car. "I'm fine— and I didn't. Let's get inside and I'll tell you all about it." She lay her hand on Hannah's shoulder, allowing Hannah's anxious breath to escape.

While Dawn stripped off her wet jacket and shoes, Hannah microwaved a bowl of the chicken stir-fry she'd made earlier.

With her feet encased in slippers and a calm expression on her face, Dawn sat opposite Hannah at the table and wrapped her hands around the warm bowl.

"Are you alright?" Hannah asked.

Dawn dug her fork in and chewed a mouthful of food before answering. "I am ... but I'm grateful you pushed me into going."

Hannah sucked in a breath. "What happened? Why are you so late?"

"I hadn't mentioned it as I didn't want to worry you … but I have been having quite a few headaches lately."

Hannah frowned and leaned forward, her mouth opening to speak.

Dawn held up a hand. "Let me finish before you say anything." She swallowed another mouthful of dinner while Hannah tapped her foot impatiently.

"The first thing they did was send me next door for blood to be taken—luckily, the receptionist said I was to come in before I ate or drank anything. Anyway, then I had a chat with the doctor, and he arranged an appointment for me to go to Auckland for an MRI."

"What?" Hannah gaped at her mother. "Why?"

"Because of the headaches, apparently." Dawn shrugged. "He didn't expect I would get in so quickly, but someone had cancelled this morning, so they said if I drove straight there, they would fit me in at one o'clock. So I did."

"And?"

"The entire process only took half an hour. It took much longer to find somewhere to park and then wait my turn." She waved a hand. "Then the paperwork and changing into a gown before they slid me into the tunnel thingy. I lay there thinking about things while the machine made an ungodly racket. And then it was over." She shrugged and ate another couple of mouthfuls of dinner. "Gosh, the city is so busy now. I don't know how I ever lived there."

Hannah huffed. "You should have rung me. I could have come into town and driven you."

"There was no time for that. Anyway, I'm not totally useless." There was a sharpness to her voice that Hannah hadn't heard for a long time, and she nodded knowingly. Her mother's prickly tone frequently emerged when she'd encountered a Weta or had to hold a jittery horse while she or her father mounted it —and Hannah knew it meant fear.

She breathed out slowly and gave her mother a gentle smile. "So what happened after the tests? You didn't come straight home?"

"Not immediately. I popped over to Susan and George's and had lunch with them. Of course I didn't tell them why I was there—just said I had to pick something up for the farm rather than pay a high delivery fee."

"Oh—and then?"

"Well, I must have stayed a little too long, and I didn't realise how busy the traffic gets in the afternoon. Then there was an accident on the western motorway, so it took me two hours to get back to Helensville. There was no point going to see the doctor again. He told me it could be a couple of days before he gets the results of both the blood tests and the MRI."

Hannah slumped back in her chair. "And he didn't give you any hint of what he was investigating?"

Dawn lay her fork on the empty plate. "Not really. He just growled at me for not coming to see him sooner and said it was best he check everything thoroughly." She shrugged. "So, what's been happening here?"

Hannah took a few seconds to push her concerns to the back of her mind and change the subject. "When we sell the run-off and get the accounts completed, I'm going to buy one of those four-wheel-drive buggy things to take hay around the farm."

Dawn raised her eyebrows. "Ooh, I like them. The Bennetts have got a couple. They seem kinder to the ground, especially when it's so muddy."

"Exactly. The tracks still have to be gravelled, but we'll wait until summer to do that—and do maintenance on some culverts." Hannah groaned. Every day seemed to reinforce how much work was required around the farm just to exist, never mind making life more manageable—and profitable.

Have we made the right decision?

CHAPTER 13

Dawn collected the used plates while Hannah headed for the office, casting a glance over her shoulder at her mother. It was so good to see her back to her old self. Her tests had revealed alarmingly high cholesterol while the MRI report listed small-vessel damage as the cause for her headaches and forgetfulness. As a result, Dawn was now on medication for both issues and appeared to have forgiven Hannah for her insistence that she have a check-up.

It was winter and a week of dry days had finally arrived, with clear blue skies, and an opportunity for the ground to dry a little.

Dawn popped her head around the kitchen door. "I forgot to tell you that Ed wants to move the bees here as soon as possible. I understand he's got Justin lined up to help. And I think two neighbours. All we've got to do is use our truck to transport the hives," Dawn said. "It seems Justin's having no trouble getting work around the district. Ed said you have to book him well in advance."

Hannah shrugged. "He's a hard worker."

"Seems that way. Not just at shearing, either. Ed reckons he's pretty good at carpentry and anything else asked of him."

"I wonder if he can ride a horse?" Hannah pondered. "We need to draft the final herd of cattle and pick out the best hundred cows to bring home from the run-off. Once that's done, we can send the rest to the sale yards." She paused. "Which reminds me ... have you heard any more from the agent? Does the prospective buyer know yet that we're happy to accept his offer—when the time comes?"

"Apparently so. I'll give the solicitor a call later and get his opinion."

"Great. Thanks, Mum. I'll leave you to have that discussion while I ring Ed about the bees."

As Hannah dropped the pad and pen on the desk, a glance out the window revealed a familiar blue utility driving into the Fantail Ridge yard. Her heart leapt. She hadn't seen Justin since Ed's birthday party six weeks before. Her pulse raced.

Hissing, "Justin's here," at her mother, she walked through the kitchen to the back door. "I'll go." She ignored her mother's knowing smile.

The gate squeaked, and Hannah grimaced.

Oh yeah, another job—oil those hinges.

"Gidday, Hannah. How're you going?"

"Good thanks." She cleared her throat. "You?"

"Great. Been busy, but that's good."

Hannah fidgeted with her long hair, wishing she'd washed it the previous night. Instead, she'd sat up late reading and left it too late to get her mop dry before bed. Not that it mattered of course. She wasn't interested in Justin.

"Ed wants us to move the bees tonight—if that suits you, of course?" he said.

"Great." She grinned. "It's been a while since we discussed the subject. I thought he'd want them shifted during the rain—to ensure they'd all be tucked up nice and tight inside the hives before we move them."

"Right." Justin smiled, his dark eyes sparkling.

Hannah's breath caught.

"So the truck. I'm guessing you want me to drive out there tonight. What time?"

"No," he said.

Hannah's eyes widened in surprise.

"Sorry. I don't mean to wreck your plans. I thought, seeing as there are only four hives and the back of my ute is big enough, I'll take the canopy off and load them on the tray—and bring them here for you. Ed will be with me, of course, and the other fellas will follow if we need them. But I reckon we'll manage without the truck."

Relieved to not have to tackle the slippery, muddied road in the dark, Hannah grinned. "Super. Um ... would you like to come in for a cuppa?"

"No, thanks. I'm fencing over at the Andersons' at the moment, and we need to make the most of the wonderful weather. We should be here around seven. It's pitch dark by then and the bees should be well and truly home."

His gaze switched away from Hannah as Dawn came up behind her, pink hat jammed on her head despite the winter weather.

"Hello Justin. Come in."

"No, thanks, Mrs Simpson. I've got to be getting back to the Andersons' place."

"Dawn, please. Don't call me Mrs Simpson."

His face lit up and he nodded. "Okay, Dawn. Thanks again." He flicked his hand in a small wave. "See you tonight."

Hannah nodded and followed him to the gate. Red was hanging half out of the canopy window, and she moved toward him. "I'd better give your mate a quick pat seeing as he's so interested." She ruffled the dog's ears, ducking as he attempted to lick her face. "You big softie. Hello to you, too."

When Justin started the engine, she stepped back and raised a hand in farewell.

Finding herself still smiling as she walked back inside, a wave of guilty excitement touched her—ever so briefly.

———

DELIGHTED TO SEE THE NEW RAMS CONTENTEDLY grazing among the flock of a hundred proven ewes, Hannah opened the gate and waited while Lass scurried around behind them, directing the mob into the fresh paddock.

"That didn't take long. Let's head up to the ridge and see what's going on," she said to the dog as she mounted Cruiser.

She swung the gelding to the west and rode up the track toward the highest point on the farm. His flanks heaving, Cruiser stopped willingly at the top and dipped his head, running the reins through Hannah's fingers. This curious habit of his had worried Hannah initially. However, as their bond grew, she realised the horse had adjusted to her leg commands quickly and preferred being ridden on a loose rein. He showed no sign of pulling or disobedience, and Hannah reminded herself to email Kevin later with a progress report on both Delight and Cruiser.

To the west, the Tasman Sea sparkled in the sunlight while to the east, the Kaipara Harbour was calm, its surface barely rippling. A gentle, chilly breeze filtered up the hill, and Hannah zipped her jacket higher.

She let out a slow breath and touched her nose. It was cold, and she smiled. This spot had always been her favourite. Collecting the reins, she rode across the ridge, looking down at the plantation of trees her parents had planted when she was a baby. Lupins covered the ground beneath the trees and would soon be flowering. Remembering her mother's comment about missing the flowers after having to part with the run-off, Hannah paused, narrowing her eyes.

Should we be planting more? Is there a market for them—or a use I'm unaware of?

Urging Cruiser down the hill, she reached the gully and kicked him into a canter. She couldn't wait to get home, open her computer, and investigate the opportunities growing the perennial might provide.

———

DARKNESS HAD FALLEN TWO HOURS BEFORE DAWN cast another impatient glance at the clock.

"Justin said seven, but I suppose eight isn't too bad. I imagine they would have driven slowly," she said.

At the sound of a rumbling engine outside, Hannah raced for the door.

Justin.

She beckoned him through the gates, walking ahead of the dimmed headlights.

Both he and Ed wore overalls, and Justin handed Hannah a hat and veil before pulling one over his own head. They moved to the back of the ute and dropped the tailgate.

"You direct us, Ed," Justin commanded. "Hannah and I'll manoeuvre."

Calling, "Righto," Ed strolled toward the garden with Dawn. "Won't be a minute. Just need to check the area to make sure they'll be happy."

Hannah turned to Justin. "You've obviously handled bees before?"

"A couple of times—but I'm no expert. I've learned more from Ed in the past couple of months than I thought possible."

After Ed and Dawn returned, Hannah took the gloves from her pocket and jumped onto the tray beside Justin.

"The site you've prepared is perfect, Dawn." At the sound of Ed's calm tones, the butterflies in Hannah's stomach settled, and she smiled into the dark. "Those hedges will keep the wind off the hives," he continued, "and you've certainly got enough flowering shrubs and plants to provide food year round. "We're ready now. It's over to you two young ones." Ed waved his hand at Justin and Hannah and moved toward them.

It took only thirty minutes of careful manoeuvring to get the hives off the ute and positioned in the new site. Hannah breathed a sigh of relief as she stared at the four towers.

Under torch light, Ed inspected each hive and nodded his approval.

Hannah's chest squeezed when she noticed how frail he appeared next to Justin's strong, lithe body.

Taking care to keep her tone upbeat, she said, "Thank you, Ed. This is a very generous thing for you to do. I promise I will look after them as best I can."

"Of course you will, Han."

"Come and have a hot cup of cocoa now," Dawn insisted.

As they walked toward the house, Hannah stripped off her gloves and tucked them in her pocket. A hand brushed against hers, startling her. *Justin.* Shock waves shot up her arm, setting her cheeks aflame and her feet stumbling. Lurching closer to Ed, she clutched his arm to help him into the kitchen, all the while aware of Justin's gaze on her.

Her heart thumped faster and harder, and she barely registered the conversation occurring at the kitchen table.

She had made no suggestive moves toward Justin— or had she?

No. Of course not.

And, apart from being friendly and—unconsciously allowing his hand to brush against hers this evening, he had shown no interest in her for weeks.

She chewed her lip.

The hand-brush must've had been unintentional— and as such, meant nothing. Why then did she feel like a nervous sixteen-year-old?

———

As she and Dawn said goodbye to the men half an hour later, Hannah sighed. Forcing her mind away from the visitors, she left her mother at the back door and took the torch to check on the bees. The white hives shone like pillars in the light.

Good. All is well.

Brushing her hand against the soft lavender bush, she wandered inside. Her mind bounded back to her time at university—and the paper she had written on producing lavender for oil. As though someone had switched a light bulb on, she forgot about Justin and hurried to her bedroom.

Rifling through the shelf in her wardrobe where she'd stashed a pile of assignments, books on plant and food research, and a myriad of unnecessary leftovers from her study days, she found what she was looking for.

"Uh-huh!" She pulled out the purple folder and lay it on her dressing table. After shoving everything else back inside the cupboard, she flung herself on her bed and began reading.

"Goodnight, Han." Dawn's face popped around the half-open door, startling her.

She checked her watch.

Ten past ten—already?

"Night, Mum. Sleep well."

After showering and brushing her teeth, Hannah lay in bed for what seemed like hours with plans and excitement buzzing around her head. Her research into cropping lupins had not provided the ideas she had hoped for—but had she stumbled on a better option?

Lavender. Of course!

We have the land for growing a crop, and it'd be the perfect companion planting for the bees.

This could be the diversification win-win I've been chasing ...

CHAPTER 14

The following morning, Hannah rose before the sun peeped over the horizon, dressed quickly, and raced outside to feed and check on the horses. Most of the mud had dried, and the ground was firm. She let both Delight and Cruiser out of their stables to graze, grinning as they trotted to the far end of the paddock, halted, and dropped their heads. It had been years since her parents had bothered keeping a house cow, and it pleased her the area, so close to the stables, could now be dedicated to the horses.

As bitumen had replaced the gravel road into town, her mother now shopped weekly. They stored extra milk in the freezer that rumbled in the boot room, its motor generating a warm spot for the dogs to squabble over. The extra work of milking a cow when there was so much else to do was unnecessary, and Hannah was thankful for that.

She headed back to the kitchen, halting for a few moments to enjoy the yellow and orange rays fanning across the eastern sky. *No pink today. Good—another fine one, if the old tales are true.*

Dawn yawned as she entered the kitchen, sniffing the air and closing her eyes. "Yum. Porridge."

"Yep—oats with grated apple, cinnamon, and brown sugar. Sound okay?" Hannah said.

"Sounds delicious. I'll make the tea."

While Dawn scraped the last spoonful from her bowl, Hannah shared her ideas from the previous night.

"Hmm. Lavender. It might work." Dawn narrowed her eyes and faced Hannah. "Are you sure it wouldn't be too much for you, though?"

"No, I'm not—yet. I thought I'd pop out to Ed's and have a chat. He's always so practical with these sorts of things. Now we know how much we're getting for the run-off, and how much our ongoing debt will be, it's time to do a budget and work out which stream of farming will require what—and what is going to return the best income."

Hannah shoved her chair back and hurried to her room, returning within seconds with her notebook and pen. "I did a few calculations last night, and I reckon this farm will easily support a hundred cows, with the required bulls and addition of calves, of course. Two and a half thousand sheep will be a conservative number to stick with, allowing sufficient feed for lambs and any weather events that might affect the land. Then we've got the horses, and I reckon we could plant about one hectare of lavender without having a problem—Angustifolia and Intermedia."

Confusion wrinkled Dawn's face for a moment. Hannah waited while her mother absorbed her suggestions—then returned her smile. "You could be right. I love lavender and have always wanted to grow a bit more around the garden. I think, next to roses and lupins, it's my favourite plant," Dawn said.

"It could be quite a lot of work though, and I'm not sure how much will be involved in extracting the oil. The only information I can find seems to deal with ginormous commercial crops—nothing like what we would consider. That's why I want to talk to Ed. You know how clever he is with stuff. He'll probably have a few ideas."

Dawn rubbed her hands together. "Oh, this is exciting. Perhaps I could make lavender bags and heat packs, and we could sell them at the craft shop in town. Oh! We could even make lavender-scented candles. Those soy candles are all the rage these days," her mother said knowledgeably, and Hannah stifled a giggle.

"Whoa. You're way ahead of me. First, we'd have to fence off the section of land. Can't have stock getting in and trampling the plants. While that's happening, I'll have to source seedlings, or buy seeds and get them started now, because they need to be in the ground by spring if we're going to have a summer harvest."

"Right then, my girl. You'd best be moving. I'll clean up here and do my chores. Will you be home for lunch?"

"I expect so. Today's Tuesday, and I think the district nurse comes to help Ed, doesn't she?"

"Yes. Tuesday, Thursday, and Saturday mornings—more than he wants, but I think we've finally convinced him he's not a spring chicken anymore."

Hannah giggled and hugged her mother. "See you later."

———

PULLING THE WOODEN GARDEN CHAIR CLOSER, HANNAH leaned her elbows on the table and studied the old man. Despite the winter sun glinting on the teapot, the breeze was cold and Hannah wrapped her hands around her mug.

"I think it's a good idea." Ed rubbed his chin, his eyes narrowing. "Of course, you can't expect a return for a year or two. We know what a gamble farming is, but I think, if you're patient, this could be an excellent investment."

"Thanks, Bestefar." Hannah covered his gloved hand with hers. "I know it will be a tough beginning but I'm prepared for that—and the extra work."

They sat for a few minutes in silence.

Hannah drew herself up. "At least the debt will be manageable once the land sale goes through. And I'll be doing what you have always said is a good thing—putting my eggs in several baskets."

He leaned forward, resting his hands on the top of his walking stick. "That, and an open mind, will certainly help. We both know you've got the determination—and the knowledge."

Hannah and the older man shared a smile before she gave him a hug. "I'll make us a fresh pot of tea, shall I? Then I'd better go home and get this show on the road."

The old man nodded, his blue eyes bright—and a wave of love for him flowed through Hannah.

———

THE MINUTE SHE ARRIVED HOME, HANNAH PICKED UP the phone and dialled several plant nurseries in her search for lavender. Satisfied it was the right time of year to try both seedlings and seeds, she ordered and paid a deposit. Checking both her personal bank balance and that of the farm account, her heart sank. It was a daunting experience to see one in the red and the other emptying frighteningly fast.

Her insides tensed as she studied the calendar. Only eleven more days before settlement day—and still so much to do. The remaining cattle needed to be mustered, weighed, and sorted. Some would be sent to the weekly sale, and those that they selected to keep, walked from the run-off to the home farm. The remaining hay in the shed had to be loaded onto the truck, brought home and restacked—and she had promised the agent she would do a final check of every boundary fence before handover.

Next, she dialled Justin's mobile, relieved when it went straight to message bank. She wasn't sure how she felt about him—confused? However, she'd already witnessed his capabilities and work ethic, and Fantail Ridge needed him. This was not the time to consider any other emotion.

"Lunch is ready." Dawn threw another log on the fire as she spoke, and Hannah grinned at her.

"Thanks. I'm starving." Hannah pointed to the wood basket. "Have we got enough to last the winter?"

"Yes, thank goodness. One thing your father was efficient with was keeping the wood heap well stocked. I expect it will be two or three years before we need to worry about it."

Hannah huffed. With everything else on the farm to consider, she had barely registered the stacked wood that filled the woodshed and stretched along the fence line behind the house.

"I quite enjoy chopping kindling and carting fire-wood. It keeps me fit—and I always wear gloves and long sleeves in case I spot a Weta!" Dawn pulled a face, and Hannah sympathised with her. The giant flightless crickets were endemic to New Zealand and, although harmless, their desire to hide amongst the wood heap meant they could give unsuspecting wood collectors quite a fright. Hannah was sure they took great delight in startling visitors—particular her and her mother.

Hannah ate quickly, keen to make the most of the pleasant weather.

"Do you want to come with me, Mum?" she asked as she dropped her spoon in the empty bowl. "I'm going to have a good look at the top part of the old bull paddock where the slope is gentle. I'll do a soil test there, and also one in the paddock across the road. Both would be okay, I reckon, but the bull paddock's easier to access for us and closer to the house. It's always drained well and should be suitable for lavender."

"Of course. Shall we take a few star pickets and a roll of wire and mark it out at the same time?"

Hannah chuckled. "I bet Dad would laugh at that comment if he was here. I can even hear him. 'Look at our farmer go! You'd never recognise the determined city girl who arrived here forty years ago—hadn't seen a cow close-up and was terrified of horses.'"

Even though Dawn still wasn't exactly in love with the big four-legged equines, she was confident and capable in every other way—and Hannah was so proud of her.

"Good idea. It's times like this we could do with one of those little 'cargo all-terrain vehicles'—or ATVs, as they call them," Hannah said.

"Ooh—you have been studying, haven't you? Yes, I agree. Let's buy one as soon as we can afford it. Today, though, I suppose Little Red will have to do."

The two women donned jackets and boots before heading outside and sliding the heavy door to the machinery shed open. Inside was a long, sturdy workbench, complete with a wall of tools, a drill press, and a vice. Lengths of building timber and corrugated iron, rolls of wire, boxes of fencing staples, cans of paint and drums of oil filled a wall of shelving which divided the workshop from the rest of the shed. A smaller row of shelves covered the end wall and contained every other imaginable piece of farm equipment.

Two vehicle bays occupied the right-hand side of the dividing shelves, one currently housing the farm truck and the other, an ancient red International Harvester tractor that had been servicing the farm's needs for almost two generations. Attached to the rear of the vehicle was a small carrier tray just big enough to hold a few bales of hay or a quantity of fencing materials required for repairs.

Both Dawn and Hannah loved 'Little Red', despite the sometimes cantankerous starter motor, which could take up to five minutes to kick into life. It was compact to manoeuvre and, with its roll bars and sturdy roof to keep off the worst of any rain, both women felt safe.

Hannah busily began stacking posts onto the tractor.

"What do you think—wire or this roll of electric tape?" Dawn called.

"We'll take the electric tape. Today is really only to get an idea of the area we need. This will do for now." Hannah lay the post ram on top of the pickets and climbed into the seat.

While the engine whirred into life, Dawn took the dogs away from the shed so Hannah could reverse out. Fluffy white clouds dotted the blue sky, and a stiff wind blew off the sea as they puttered down the track.

An hour later, with the soil tests confirming the old bull paddock had the perfect pH balance, Hannah bashed in the corner posts. Striding back and forth from the tractor to the row of tape laying in a straight line on the grass, Dawn placed the star pickets ready to be driven into the ground.

"Gosh. It looks an enormous area." Dawn grimaced. "That's a lot of bending over planting and weeding."

"It's less than a hectare, Mum. I think it will be perfect." Hannah laughed, excitement bubbling inside her. "Now we take the carrier off and put the little plough on, and I'll keep myself busy for the rest of the afternoon—and probably most of tomorrow too."

"Okay. Let's do it." Dawn's enthusiasm matched Hannah's, and she straightened her shoulders. "This is a whole new beginning for us both."

CHAPTER 15

Hannah was dozing in the armchair when Justin returned her call at nine o'clock that evening.

"Sorry I missed your call. I was fencing out on the coast today. No reception." His voice was bright but slower than usual. Hannah sympathised. *You're tired.*

"That's okay. This is random, but I was wondering if you can ride a horse?"

"I can. Haven't for a while but I did a fair bit of it in Australia. Some jobs out there in the outback are tricky in the wet—and the station I was on preferred to use horses, anyway."

"Great. I was calling to see if you have a few days spare to give us a hand here?"

"Sure. When?"

"Some time in the next week, if possible. We've got a couple of things going on because of the land sale. I want to bring the last of the cattle home and could do with another rider. I've booked the carrier to come and take the stock we decide not to keep which will leave us around a hundred or more. Mum will drive the truck ahead of us once we've got the cattle together and can head home. Because of having to travel along public roads for a bit, I don't want to risk anything going wrong."

"That'll be fine. I'll finish the current job on the weekend. Would Monday suit?"

"Perfect. Thanks. I'll have a horse ready for you if you don't mind leaving your ute here. We'll ride over."

"Okay—and the second job?"

"Oh, I nearly forgot. There's no urgency because I haven't received the plants yet—but I'm putting in a small plantation of lavender and would appreciate another pair of hands to get the area fenced and then get the seedlings in the ground."

"Interesting. Lavender, hey? Can't say I've had much to do with it, but I'm happy to help. What do you do with it?"

"Um—well, at this stage, I hope to use the buds for lavender bags, heat packs, soap. You know, crafty type stuff. We will harvest the rest for oil."

There was a pause before Justin replied, and Hannah wondered what he was thinking. *Are you laughing at me, or thinking I'm nuts?*

"Sounds interesting. How do you extract the oil?"

"Via a steam still—which I haven't yet figured out how to get a hold of, but I'm working on that. Meanwhile, there'll be two different seedlings to plant in hilled rows—sort of like potatoes. I'd like to allocate each species separate ends of the field so I can compare their growth—and, of course, for ease of harvesting."

"Sure. I'll be in on that. Let's get the cattle sorted and put the fence up. Once that's done, I can give you a hand to get the rows set up or whatever you want."

She pictured his muscles rippling and bit her lip. "It-it could involve a fair bit of shovelling by hand."

He laughed. "I'm sure I'll manage whatever's needed."

"Good. Appreciate that. See you next Monday then?"

"Will do."

Hannah lay back in the chair with her hands behind her head. Tomorrow she would finish ploughing the furrows. She'd need to be careful. Allowing the tyres to crush the grass between rows would only create more work—and weeding. It had taken a while to calculate the distance needed, but she believed she'd got it right. What she wanted now was for the weather to remain dry enough to keep the soil firm. *Working in pouring rain and boggy ground will not work at all.*

———

THE FOLLOWING MORNING DAWNED, COLD AND DRIZZLY. Hannah trawled through the met report, breathing a sigh of relief that the forecast rain would not hang around. By mid-morning, she hoped conditions would be just right for preparing the soil.

Delighted that the weather prediction was spot on for a change, Hannah returned to the plot of ground before lunch and continued puttering up and down the rows, working the soil deeper and making it more friable with each run of the plough. Little Red chugged on, and she patted the old tractor's dashboard.

"I knew you could." She grinned, remembering how much she had loved the childhood story of *The Little Engine That Could.*

Even more ancient than the tractor, the plough was a single disk, originally pulled by a horse. Hannah's grandfather had told her Uncle Tim had modified it so it could work off the power take-off shaft at the rear of the tractor. She had thought him incredibly talented. Now, she wondered if walking behind a horse without noise and fumes—not to mention the reduced damage to the grasses between rows—wouldn't be preferable.

Eventually, she completed the last row and looked back at the rich brown furrows of earth divided by stripes of green. She pushed the lever forward to lift the plough out of the ground and drove home.

As she exited the paddock onto the track, she looked back at her work.

"Hmm, wonky, but not too bad." She grinned to herself. Grease covered her gloves, her ears were ringing despite wearing earmuffs, and her shoulders ached from the constant vibration of hanging on to the steering wheel, which had been made long before power-steering was developed.

"Thanks, Little Red. Not a bad day's work."

———

ALL WEEKEND, RAIN SLASHED THE GROUND, AND THE wind howled, rattling the windows, and blowing smoke back down the chimney into the living room. Apprehension festered inside Hannah as she worried about the freshly prepared ground, shifting the cattle in such unpleasant conditions, and whether she should have stuck to just sheep and cattle—and not tried to diversify. It was all so stressful!

To distract herself, she spent the two days sorting and clearing out the machinery shed. Years of accumulated dust rose, filling Hannah's nose and turning her hair a pale shade of gold. She transferred the truck to the empty hay shed in the paddock across the road. Coughing noisily, she dragged the timber and sheets of iron to the empty truck bay. By the end of the weekend, she stood back and plastered a satisfied smile on her face.

She picked Scruffy up and held him against her, swivelling around in a slow circle as rain pattered on the tin roof. "What do you think? Will it fit the bill as a potential lavender-processing plant? Once we get the still installed and find some tables and whatever else we'll need, of course."

The little dog licked her chin and squirmed. She lowered him to the ground again and stood outside under the awning of the building. The rain had eased, leaving puddles glimmering in the late afternoon sun that peeped between the clouds. A family of magpies warbled, their melodic song sparking joy as they perched above her on the power line. Hannah grinned at them before looking down at Scruffy.

"Come on, little fellow. We'd better see to the horses and lock Mum's chooks up for her."

Scruffy wagged his tail furiously and leapt on top of Lass, who had spent the afternoon asleep on a sack in the corner. The Border Collie staggered to her feet, raising her head and turning it away from her annoying canine friend.

Hannah patted Lass, holding each side of her face gently. "Yes, we'll feed you too—and Jet."

Trailing around the compound and stables, she felt like the Pied Piper as the three dogs, her father's stock horse, and one fat pony followed her. She led Delight from her stable and let her loose in the knee-deep grass of the paddock beside the house, then installed Monty in the empty stall next to Cruiser. Then, after mixing horse nuts and chaff together, she tipped the mixture into the feed bins and moved toward the hay nets to fill them. "You two will have a big day tomorrow, so you'd better enjoy your tea and have a good rest."

She turned to look at Honeysuckle. The pony nickered and rubbed her face against Hannah, shoving her in the stomach with her head. "As for you, my little pudding, I think you can have a night in the yard next to your boyfriends on a diet of fresh air and moonlight."

Minutes later, Hannah stripped off her filthy clothes and stood under the warm shower. Dirt ran in rivulets down the drain, and she watched it flow before tilting her head back and lathering her hair with shampoo. Her thoughts raced forward to tomorrow and her stomach fluttered. After a ride around the boundaries, removing all the cattle from the property would be the last step in saying goodbye to the land that had been in the family for a generation. She had played on it, ridden every square metre of it, picked bunches of lupins from it—and as she grew older, she had worked hard on it alongside her parents. Her last job would be to shift the cattle to the home farm, leaving the expanse of reclaimed sand hills, rough gullies, and rolling pastures to the new owner. She knew she should be sad, but deep down, she wasn't. She had always known it was a piece of land originally bought to help the family prosper through the trials of the 1970s and 80s. On the whole, it had worked. However, the burden it had obviously placed on her father made Hannah's heart ache. The decision was the right one.

CHAPTER 16

Breathing a sigh of relief, Hannah threw back the bedcovers and opened the window. Cold air blasted through the room, and she hastily closed it again. *At least it's not raining.*

Bolting her breakfast, Hannah ran through the day's plan with her mother while she drained her mug.

"Don't worry, love. I'll be fine. You concentrate on getting the horses ready and I'll nip over to the hay shed and bring the truck back here so I can pack a picnic lunch for us all. I'll bring the dogs with me so they're not worn out before you get there—and I promise I'll meet you at the cattle yards at ten o'clock. Happy?"

Hannah gave Dawn a quick hug. "Of course. Thanks, Mum. Justin said he'd be here early, so I'm guessing that means he could be here any minute." She grabbed her warm jacket from the hook by the door and pulled on her riding boots.

A series of snorts and whinnies greeted her as she neared the stables, and she laughed. "Good boys. I'll give you some breakfast while I get you ready."

She removed their rugs and groomed both geldings. Cruiser's hair was fine and soft with a shine that brought out the gold flecks in his rich bay coat, whereas Monty's was thick and much longer, requiring a stiff brush and currycomb. She lifted the saddle onto Monty's back. A vehicle rumbled closer. Hannah's pulse raced. It pulled into the yard and the engine stilled.

"I'm over here. In the stables!" Hannah yelled and waved from the railing.

Wrapped in a thick tartan jacket and with a woollen hat pulled down to his eyebrows, Justin waved back and strode toward her. Hannah glanced at his footwear, relieved to see sturdy boots with a heel.

"Here's your trusty steed. His name's Monty and he was Dad's, so he's used to having a man ride him. You shouldn't have any trouble."

"I'm sorry about your dad, Hannah. When did he pass away?"

"In March. It was a shock to us all. Cancer. An aggressive one."

His face softened and he stepped toward her. She hastily pulled her riding helmet on and passed her father's to Justin.

"You probably didn't wear one of these in Aussie, but here, it has always been one of the most important rules, and I never ride without one."

Justin nodded, pulling the woollen hat off and shoving it into his pocket. "Actually, we did. The station owner insisted on them. They'd had a few mishaps in the past and with litigation the way it is now, he didn't want to take chances." He wriggled the helmet over his thick, dark hair and raised his chin to adjust the strap. "Feels like your dad's brains were about the same size as mine."

Hannah grinned, closed the gate behind them, and led Cruiser alongside Monty. "Ready?"

"I reckon I am."

This will be interesting. Hannah watched with surprise as Justin swung his leg over the saddle and picked up the reins as if he did it every day. Her eyes widened. *Good start.*

"What? You thought I might have forgotten how to ride?"

Hannah blushed. "Perhaps."

As she put her foot in the stirrup, Dawn called from the house gate. "See you at the yards at ten."

"Thanks, Mum. See you then."

The first twenty minutes were slow as they negotiated their way through the smaller fields, opening and shutting gates while the horses warmed up and lengthened their stride. Reaching the hundred-acre paddock that ran along a ridge at the back of the farm, Hannah called out, "We'll have to canter here or it'll take us forever to get there."

In a heartbeat, Monty lengthened his stride, loping calmly beside Cruiser. The big thoroughbred increased his pace. Wind whipped through Hannah's hair, tendrils flicking her face. Monty failed to keep up. For the first time since she'd brought the horse home, Hannah had to shorten her reins.

"He must think we're on the racetrack!" Her voice rose above the wind as it whistled over the top of the ridge, and she caught Justin's understanding glance out of the corner of her eye. He dropped back and Cruiser immediately eased his pace, content with being the leader.

At the far corner of the home farm, Hannah dismounted and hooked the boundary gate open, tying it securely to the fence with a piece of wire attached for that purpose.

"This is the way we'll come back and for the moment, the plan is to leave the cattle here to settle. They've got the bush down the bottom for shelter, and there's plenty of water in this paddock." Hannah waved an arm in a sweeping gesture.

Aware of Justin's gaze following her every movement, she tensed. Why couldn't she think of anything to say?

"I gather you don't have a boyfriend at the moment?"

Surprised, Hannah spun her gaze to meet his lazy smile. She huffed and urged Cruiser into a trot.

"So is that a yes or a no?" Monty drew alongside her again, with Justin leaning forward, his expression serious now.

"It's a no." She dropped back to a walk and shrugged. "I had one for nearly four years while I was at the research station. Things didn't work out—and I'm too busy and disillusioned to bother, even if there was a nice, hardworking, kind, and understanding man right under my nose." Her heart thumped in her chest. *I shouldn't have said that. Now he'll think he's nice and hardworking and kind and understanding and ... oh Lord. He'll think I'm interested in him.*

"You?" she asked as she fiddled with Cruiser's mane.

"Nah. Got too used to my company now—and I enjoy it."

"You're not exactly over the hill yet though, are you?"

He grunted. "I'm thirty-four. Old enough to know I won't be going down the same road as my parents—or my dumb-arsed uncles."

Ah. That's a good sign—isn't it? She met his gaze, seeing the sheer unbridled honesty in his eyes and knew he was telling the truth.

The end of the public lane adjoining the road to the run-off was in sight, and they had a job to do. Hannah would have liked to delve deeper, but this was not the time. She'd already discovered a little of Justin's family.

The last thing she wanted to do was to open her mouth and put her foot in it.

————

MUSTERING THE CATTLE WAS EASIER THAN HANNAH HAD expected. With the main herd sheltering in the lea of the ridge out of the westerly winds, it took less than half an hour to ride around the perimeter of the paddock and collect the stragglers.

With the stock penned in the paddock beside the yards, Hannah and Justin dismounted, tied their horses to the yard rail, and joined the waiting Dawn for a hot drink and a cheese scone.

"So far, so good?" Dawn asked.

Hannah gave her the thumbs-up sign as she chewed her mouthful.

"You've got some nice cattle here, ladies." Justin angled his head, studying the herd. "I reckon if this lot were in outback Australia, the buyers would fight over them."

"Well, lucky they're not. We've spent quite a lot of time selecting the best from all we had a couple of months ago. Now we have to hope our selection process is justified." Hannah grimaced as she answered and held up crossed fingers. Dawn shot Justin an appreciative smile.

Minutes later, Jet and Lass sat beside the horses, waiting for their commands while Dawn packed up the picnic. Justin strode to the gate leading out onto the road as Hannah untied the horses and mounted Cruiser, leading Monty alongside her.

"You go ahead in the truck now, Mum. Keep it steady, and everything should be good."

"Of course, dear. Remember, I have done this once or twice—including before you were even born." Dawn shot Hannah a grin.

"Sorry. I'll try to focus my bossiness on the dogs." Hannah laughed and swung the horses toward the back of the cattle and waited.

The procession began slowly, with the truck leading the way through the open gateway. Justin stood back, well clear of the moving herd, while Hannah called out.

"Speak up, Jet!" she cried. The Huntaway's deep bark echoed from the surrounding hills and the cattle moved off in a rush.

Weaving the horses back and forth, Hannah talked constantly to the mob. "Steady girls, steady! Whoa." Lass dropped to the ground, eyeing a recalcitrant cow who stamped her hoof, considered the dog, and finally turned to trot after her companions.

Once through the gate, the big red and white bovines seemed to reorganise themselves and dropped to a steady walk. A couple of younger heifers frisked and bunted each other as if excited about their newfound freedom.

Hannah waited while Justin closed the gate before taking Monty's reins from her and quickly mounting.

"Righto, partner. We're in business," Justin said, shooting Hannah an infectious grin.

"I sure hope so." She flashed a quick smile while trying to keep her eyes on the herd—and attempting to contain the excitement that fizzed in her veins.

The trek was slow as the cows snatched at mouthfuls of grass from the roadside, enjoying their outing. At the junction of the main road and the track leading to the home farm, Dawn had parked the truck crosswise and was standing in the middle of the gravel, her bright pink hat a beacon while she waved her arms like a traffic controller. Without hesitation, the lead cow glanced at her and turned down the track. The junction was the only part of the ride between the two farms that ever caused problems. Once through it and headed for home, Hannah knew all would be well, and she breathed a sigh of relief.

As both cattle and humans eased into a rhythm, Hannah swivelled her gaze around their surroundings. From the ridge track they were offered a 360 degree panorama. To their left, lush green pastures flowed down to the harbour while on their right, rough grasses and toe-toe led to a pine tree plantation before meeting the vast Tasman Sea. In front of them, the land rolled gently southward, dotted with houses, sheds, and swathes of trees and manuka.

"Pretty awesome view, isn't it?"

Justin nodded. "It certainly is. It's hard to believe I am enjoying a ride in such a beautiful place—not to mention being in the company of a pretty incredible woman."

Hannah jerked her gaze toward him as heat rose on her neck. "Don't be stupid." She squirmed with embarrassment. If she had ever had tickets on herself, they had been well and truly squashed by Todd. Her long, gangly limbs, auburn hair, and freckled face were not exactly model material—and he had reminded her regularly of that.

"You're more attractive than you think you are, Hannah Simpson."

She turned her head away, dismissing his comment while she beat herself up over her extended relationship with Todd. Why had she hung around with him for so long? She'd been stupid, naïve, and too inexperienced to recognise Todd's narcissistic tendencies and what he was doing to her.

Dropping back a few strides, she studied Justin from behind. His back was straight and relaxed in the saddle, his hands gentle on the reins, and his long legs immobile against Monty's sides, completely at one with the horse. She frowned. He certainly had showed no sign of having inherited his father's violent temper —nor had he shown either Dawn or her any disrespect. Could he really be a genuinely nice guy?

Oh, God. Since Todd, I've become suspicious and judgemental.

That was all the reminder she needed. Love wasn't worth the risk.

Look what it can do to your head—never mind your heart.

———

With the cattle safely locked in the hundred-acre paddock, Dawn headed for home via the gravelled tracks while Hannah led Justin across the countryside, checking the troughs and sheep as they went.

They were almost home when lightning cracked over the sea, and the rumble of thunder rolled overhead.

"We'd better get a wriggle on if we're to beat that," Hannah called. Without a word, Justin urged Monty into a canter and both horses galloped for home, Cruiser's nose edging ahead of Monty.

The deluge fell two minutes after they rode into the yard and only seconds behind Dawn. She had tucked the truck into the shed beside Little Red, and the three of them stood under the corrugated-iron awning, the horses' sides heaving with exertion while they all watched the rain tumble down.

"I think we'll unsaddle them here and lead them to the stables as soon as it lets up enough to not get drowned," Hannah said.

Justin nodded, laughing as Jet shook himself and sprayed everyone—including the horses. Before Hannah had undone Cruiser's girth, Justin had whipped off Monty's saddle and sat it on its pommel, leaning against the workbench.

"My mother is coming to stay for a few days," Justin said, his voice soft and uncertain.

Both Dawn and Hannah stared at him simultaneously.

"Carol?" Dawn asked.

"Yes. Carol. My mother. She's got a week off work and rang last night to tell me she wants to come and see me."

"That's great news, isn't it?" Hannah studied his blank expression as she spoke. He didn't seem overly excited about her visit, but then again, he hadn't come across as being an emotional person—so far, anyway.

"Yes, it is. We are quite close ... but I suppose after years of having Nigel doing his best to divide us, we've become pretty good at hiding our feelings. I'm really looking forward to seeing her." He hesitated, his gaze fixed somewhere out in the rain and for a few seconds, he seemed oblivious to his companions. He turned back to them. "Would you both like to come and have dinner with us while she's here? Perhaps on Friday night ... or next weekend?"

Hannah met her mother's gaze momentarily before Dawn answered, "We would love to. Perhaps I could make dessert?"

Justin's face broke into a beaming smile. "That'd be great. I'm a dab hand at a roast or barbeque, but I'm not much good on the dessert scene."

"What's your favourite?" Dawn asked.

"Lemon meringue pie."

Hannah chuckled. "It's ours too. Mum makes the best lemon meringue pie you'll ever taste."

"Well then. It's a deal." As he spoke, the rain stopped as suddenly as it had started. Drips of water formed a thin veil around the shed, falling from the gutter, but in the paddocks, the drops had stopped. "And on that note, I reckon it's time to get these horses rubbed down and fed ... and I'll head home."

Surprised to see the delight on Dawn's face, Hannah softened. Perhaps an evening in the company of this man—and her mother's old friend—was just what they both needed.

As they walked toward the house, Dawn nudged Hannah with her elbow. "It'll be lovely to see Carol again—and of course for you and Justin to spend time together that isn't about work."

"Mum! Stop trying to play Cupid."

They both giggled, linked arms, and walked inside.

CHAPTER 17

As showers continued throughout the afternoon, Hannah opened her laptop and began refreshing her knowledge of lavender farming and distilling the oil. The computer pinged as an email came through, and she flicked over to it.

Hi Hannah,

How's life? Nothing changes here—work is busy and no one has been appointed to your job yet. Maybe Brian is hanging out, hoping you'll return—ha ha? I miss you and was wondering what you're doing this weekend? I've got Friday and Monday off and thought I'd drive up to see you? Is that okay? I'll make one of my famous Irish stews with colcannon and bring it with me—to remind you of some of the fun evenings we spent with the girls before you hooked up with that dropkick Todd. Deal?

Talk soon, Ellie

Hannah grinned. She missed her funny Irish workmate even more than she missed the occasional evenings with the girls from work. Those get-togethers had been fun, with each of them bringing a dish of food to share and a bottle or two of wine, then sitting around Ellie's flat listening to music, talking, and laughing into the wee hours. Then Todd had swept her off her feet—and the next four years had become a frantic mix of riding, competing at show jumping events, working, and bowing to Todd's every demand.

She hit reply.

Great to hear from you, Ellie. Yes—I would love you to come and stay. Send me a text when you get to Helensville so I can make sure I'm home.

H

As soon as she hit send, she remembered Justin's invitation to dinner. "Blast. Now I'll have to cancel."

Dawn popped her head around the door. "Cuppa?"

"Yes, please." She frowned. "I've just had an email from Ellie, and she's coming for the weekend. I forgot about dinner at Justin's. Shall I cancel?"

"Of course not. This is the country, remember? I'm sure Justin won't mind if an extra person turns up. Ring him tomorrow and check—so he has plenty of notice."

Hannah wasn't so sure. Dinner for four seemed balanced. Adding a chirpy Irishwoman to the mix might not be quite what Carol would expect. *Will Justin think I've deliberately tried to sabotage a cosy evening with our mothers?*

She tossed and turned that night while a Morepork called outside; the sound heightened the random dreams that filled her head. When she finally woke, weary and unsettled, she could remember none of them.

———

"DON'T WORRY ABOUT IT. ANOTHER PERSON JOINING IN will be welcome."

Hannah relaxed into the comfy living room chair, the floral brocade worn under her fingertips. "Thanks, Justin. I'm sorry to dump this on you."

"Hey. I said it'll be fine. The more the merrier." He continued without a pause. "I'm taking Mum out to visit Ed tomorrow. I reckon it could be an emotional reunion for them both from what I understand."

"I'm sure he'll love that."

"I hope so. They can talk all they like tomorrow." He gave a quiet chuckle. "I'm giving Andersons a hand with a shed roof while she's with Ed. Thought it'd be nice for the two of them to have a good yarn without me."

Hannah nodded into the phone. "Sounds good. Thanks again. See you on Saturday then. About six o'clock?"

"Yeah. It's a date."

"A date?"

"I mean. Not a date. It's dinner with my mum and

your mum and your friend," Justin rushed to continue, but butterflies flitted in Hannah's stomach. Why did he have this effect on her?

"I'll see you then," Hannah said weakly as she replaced the phone in the cradle.

"All okay?"

Hannah spun around at her mother's voice and gave her a sheepish grin. "Yeah. He said, 'The more, the merrier'."

"Told you so." Dawn gave Hannah a gentle shove.

———

THE REST OF THE WEEK SEEMED TO DRAG AS RAIN continued incessantly. Hannah desperately sought out jobs to take her mind off the list of maintenance jobs. While she de-cobwebbed the soon-to-be lavender shed, scrubbed the ancient table, and welded new hinges onto the iron gate leading to the bush, she huffed impatiently. Waiting for settlement day for the run-off. Waiting for Ellie to arrive—and waiting for Saturday to come, the most nerve-wracking of all.

Hannah woke to sunshine streaming into her bedroom on Friday morning, the day of Ellie's arrival. She threw the covers back and opened the window, leaning on the sill and resting her chin on her hands. In the back garden, the steady buzz of bees working in the lavender and camelias caught her attention. She breathed in the scent of earth and pine trees after rain and smiled as a family of magpies sitting on the power line warbled to their hearts' content, as though eager to welcome her to the new day.

"Good morning, Mother Nature," Hannah said. A draft of cool winter air entered the room, and she shivered, quickly closing the window.

After dressing, she brushed her hair and tied it in its habitual ponytail, then drifted into the living room.

Dawn had risen early and dressed in her gardening clothes, was dishing up scrambled eggs. She beamed at Hannah. "Good morning. You must have been exhausted, sleeping this late."

Hannah squinted at the hands on the old timber clock that had sat on the mantlepiece since her grandparents built the house. Ten minutes past eight.

"Cripes. I didn't realise it was so late." She grinned at her mother. "Must have been that bottle of wine we knocked off last night."

Dawn chuckled. "Maybe. Did us both good though, didn't it? I haven't slept that well since before your father got sick."

They shared a smile and Hannah gave her a hug. *Good on you Mum. You've just admitted you've taken a big step in your grief.*

To celebrate the sale of the run-off and the subsequent injection of funds in the farm account, Dawn had dragged a bottle of South Island Pinot Noir from the cupboard in the sitting room the previous night.

"Better not make a habit of it then—there's too

much to do." Hannah grinned and dug into her plate of eggs.

"Is there anything you'd like to do while Ellie's here?"

Hannah inclined her head at Dawn's question. "We-ell. Considering she's never been on a New Zealand farm, I think I should take her for a walk through the bush to see the Fantails—and other birds. We might take the net down to the beach, too, and drag for mullet. What do you think?"

Dawn clapped her hands with the excitement of a child. "Perfect. We haven't had fish for ages. I'll get the smokehouse going so we can eat some fresh and smoke the rest to put in the freezer."

"Whoa. Hang on, Mother dear," Hannah quipped. "We might not catch any. I suggest you wait until we see if there are any about first. And before that, it might be a good idea to check the tides. I haven't been down to the beach since I got home, and I've no idea of tide times."

"Sorry, Han. Nor have I. Anyway, Ellie might not be interested. Okay, what else?" Dawn sat back in her chair and met Hannah's gaze.

"She's not a rider, so I can't put her on a horse to show her around. She loves dogs though, so perhaps we'll go for a walk around the farm—a bit each day so she can see the animals and enjoy the fresh air. Living in that horrible flat of hers must be hard—and boring." Hannah twisted her mouth, chewing on her bottom lip.

"Other than that, I suppose we'll talk, eat and … who knows?"

"You could always take her for a drive to Ed's place. I know he doesn't have the wild birds anymore, but his garden is still pretty amazing. June Radley comes every week, and Ed hoes away with his new weed remover at every opportunity. Anyway, you mentioned she gets homesick for her family in Ireland. Perhaps she misses her grandparents or something?" Dawn shrugged.

Hannah pushed her chair back and gathered the plates. "Good idea. She won't be here before lunchtime though, so I'm going to give each of the horses a thorough grooming and both Cruiser and Honeysuckle a workout while the weather's nice."

She pushed the gate open into the yard and gave a little skip. It was a gorgeous day. The bank account looked more positive than it had in years, and soon, her friend would be here. She had missed her more than she realised.

A welcoming whinny from the stables put a smile on Hannah's face, and she launched into giving Delight a brisk brushing before releasing her into the paddock to graze. Her leg appeared almost better with tiny, fine hairs growing back, hiding the new flesh. If only she didn't limp occasionally. In every other way, she looked exactly as she had three weeks before the Horse of the Year show.

It was after midday before Hannah had finished riding and shifted all four horses into the big paddock that ran alongside the narrow dirt road between the homestead and larger portion of the farm.

"There you go. No rain predicted for days, so you can all enjoy the spring sunshine and have a brief holiday."

She trailed back to the house, singing James Blunt's "You're Beautiful" as she wandered. Apart from a couple of fluffy white clouds, the sky was clear and, although the breeze was cool, the air was alive with bird calls and the hum of busy bees.

She breathed in the delicious smell of bacon and egg pie as she entered the kitchen. "Yum. That smells good."

Dawn threw her a glance as she bustled into the dining room with a bowl of salad and freshly sliced bread. "You'd better whip through the shower before Ellie gets here, Hannah. You smell like a horse."

Hannah chuckled. Of course she did.

CHAPTER 18

From the moment Ellie arrived, a warm, relaxed feeling encompassed Hannah—an easing of worry and responsibility.

Ellie hauled herself out of the tiny car with the tell-tale dings in the bumper and a trail of yellow paint scrapes on the passenger side. She threw her arms around Hannah.

"It's so good to see you. What a gorgeous place to live. I think I've gone home to Ireland!" Ellie babbled, her smile stretching across her round, peaches-and-cream face.

"Welcome to Fantail Ridge, Ellie. It's good to see you too." Hannah extricated herself from her friend's squishy hug. "Let me carry your bag in."

Ellie reefed open the back door and pulled out a battered backpack. "Here, you take this and I'll take the box."

Hannah peered into the cardboard carton, curious. A folded towel covered the contents, and she raised an eyebrow.

"I know you said not to, but I couldn't help myself. My mam brought me up to never turn up empty-handed—and I know how much you love my stew. So, here it is. Enough for us and your mum. All we need to do is heat it up."

"You're a gem, Ellie. Mum will love it—and so do I."

Hannah swung the backpack over her shoulder and led her friend through the white gate and onto the path leading to the back door.

"Oh, look! Jonquils." Ellie exclaimed, pausing beside the garden. "I love them. And is that a rose?" With both hands clutching the box of food, she nodded at the new foliage spreading up the lattice backdrop.

"Yes. It's an old-fashioned climber that my grandmother planted back in the 1930s. We have to chop it back each winter and usually lose a bit of skin and blood doing so, but from late spring until well into autumn, it's covered with gorgeous pink flowers. It's a bit late this year but by next month, it will look really pretty."

The back door opened and Dawn stepped toward Ellie, her arms outstretched. "It's so nice to see you again. Thank you for coming all this way."

While they hugged, Hannah smiled softly. *It's so good to be with her again.*

"Come on in. I'll put the kettle on while Hannah

shows you to your room." Dawn turned and led Ellie into the kitchen while Hannah brought up the rear.

———

IT WAS MID-AFTERNOON AND THE TWO YOUNG WOMEN had filled the hours since lunch catching up on the previous month's news while strolling around the garden. They moved to the seat under the Puriri tree and took in the serenity of Granny Alice's park. Ellie's constant chatter finally eased, and she sucked in a noisy breath and faced Hannah.

"So, tell me about this Justin that I'm destined to meet tomorrow night. Is he the new man in your life?" Ellie's face wore a cheeky grin, and Hannah shook her head fiercely.

"No, of course not. He's the tenant in our cottage and is available for casual work around the farm and shearing. That's all."

"Ah, so he's a 'useful' tenant then." Ellie snorted and gave Hannah a gentle shove. "Go on, pull the other one."

Hannah's cheeks burned, and she jumped to her feet. "Come on. You're talking rubbish now, so it's time to wear off some more energy."

Ellie had to jog to keep up with Hannah as she strode across the lawn.

Dawn was sweeping out the boot room, and the

girls skirted around the pile of gumboots and trolley of firewood sitting outside on the concrete.

"We're going for a walk through the bush, Mum. Back in an hour."

"Okay. Ellie, you might like to see if there's a pair of boots here to fit you. Those sneakers don't look like they'll handle the mud very well," Dawn said.

Hannah glanced down at Ellie's feet and grinned. "With those little twinkle toes, you'll probably have to wear the pair I had when I was about twelve."

Ellie grinned and bent to sort through the boots. She wasn't small, but compared to both the Simpson women's tall, willowy builds and long, thin feet and hands, she was definitely a little on the solid side with extremities more like those of a pre-teen.

"These feel perfect!" Ellie stamped in a circle, wearing a pair of green gumboots with pictures of horses all over them.

"They were always Hannah's favourites. That's why they're still here." Dawn laughed.

"It's true. I love them. Just wish they'd make nice boots for enormous feet instead of these boring black ones." Hannah giggled and grabbed Ellie's arm. "Come on then. At this rate, it'll be dark before we get home."

———

JUST LIKE HANNAH, ELLIE APPEARED ENTRANCED BY THE bush. The quiet, cool air filled with bird calls captured them both, and to Hannah's relief, her friend seemed to have forgotten about Justin amongst the gentle fern fronds and flittering Fantails.

"Look. Up there," Hannah whispered, and Ellie followed her gaze.

"What is it?"

"A Tui. See the tree with the yellow flowers? It's a Kowhai. They're just flowering and the Tuis love them."

They stood for a few minutes, watching the black bird with its fluffy white beard poke a long beak into each flower, extracting the nectar and any insects that dared occupy the delicate blossom.

For the next half hour, the women dawdled along the bush track. Hannah's chest swelled with pride as Ellie dished out enthusiastic praise, exclaiming excitedly as though it was the first time she had seen a native bird.

By the time they emerged from the bush at the bottom of the hill, Ellie was puffing.

"Now comes the hard bit." Hannah grinned at her friend as she pointed up the hill to where the homestead chimney was just visible behind the Norfolk Pine.

"You're a slave driver."

"Rubbish. We'll walk up the road, which is easier." Hannah set off across the grass toward the gate opening onto the road and glanced back, laughing. "You'll appreciate your dinner tonight."

———

IRISH STEW, COLCANNON, AND A BOTTLE OF RED WINE ensured all three women relaxed that evening. Hannah and Ellie shared in-house antics from the research station with Dawn before Ellie relayed snippets of life amongst of her large, emotional family, squashed together in their tiny Londonderry house.

"I noticed the piano earlier." Ellie pointed to the rich, dark timber instrument in the corner of the room. "Do you both play?"

Hannah grinned. "Mum did her best to teach me— and I tried. But if you're looking for a singalong, you'd better ask her."

Ellie turned to Dawn. "Would you mind? Please?"

"I'm sorry Ellie. I haven't played for a long time— not since John got sick. I don't think you'd enjoy it much."

"Please? I don't care if you make mistakes."

Dawn shook her head gently before giving in and moving to the piano stool.

Following a few fumbles with rusty fingers, Dawn began playing a repertoire of family favourites—songs from ABBA, Neil Diamond, John Denver, and others. Although most were from the 70s and 80s, it surprised Hannah when Ellie sang along, as familiar with every word as she was. Hannah thought she had been one of the few teenagers who enjoyed her parent's music as much as they did.

As her mother began playing "Hallelujah", Hannah's jaw dropped, and she became transfixed by her friend. Pure, melodic tones burst from Ellie's throat, rising and falling with clarity and emotion that had Hannah's arms prickling with goosebumps. When the song ended, Dawn launched into "Danny Boy". Ellie's volume increased a notch, and she closed her eyes, the pitch of her voice so passionate that Hannah thought her own heart would break. By the end of their singalong, tears flowed freely down all three faces and they sat staring at each other for what seemed like an age.

"How come I didn't know you could sing so beautifully?" Hannah asked.

Ellie shrugged. "I don't—usually. It must be this place. The house is different, but there's a feeling here that reminds me of my grandmother's cottage when I was a child. My uncles always had a gargle and a singalong. The squeeze box would come out—and the tin whistle and they'd be off."

"A gargle?" Dawn's forehead creased.

Ellie laughed. "A drink. They loved their Guinness, and music seemed to go hand in hand with it. Must be where I get it from."

As though the emotions experienced by all three women had drained them, they bid each other a solemn goodnight and headed for bed. Hannah was lost in thought.

———

Saturday dawned bright and clear with a strong westerly wind that seeped through the cracks around the windows and bent the branches of the trees.

"I think we'll have to give the mullet fishing a miss today." Hannah screwed up her face as the wind snatched the door out of her hands and it slammed shut.

"Why don't you take Ellie for a walk to the beach anyway? You'll be able to find a sheltered spot some-where … and you might even spot some delicate shells for Ellie to take home."

Hannah looked at her mother, incredulous. "Ellie's twenty-six, Mum. Not five."

Quick to react, Ellie leapt forward and put her hand on Hannah's arm. "That's a lovely idea—and if I can find a few shells to take home to decorate my bath-room, I'd be chuffed."

Hannah shrugged. "Okay. Let's do it then."

An hour later, they tramped along the overgrown track, shoving spears of flax and toe-toe out of the way until the path opened onto a patch of grass leading to the sand.

"Crikey. It's been a while since I came down here, and it doesn't look like anyone else has been either," Hannah said as she cleared the pieces of driftwood from the tiny beach and laid out a towel for them to sit on.

The wind whipped white caps across the harbour

and sand bit their legs, tossed by the gale. Seagulls swooped and dived above them, screeching.

Ellie laughed and pointed to them. "They're demanding a reason for their privacy being invaded by humans."

Hannah grinned and dragged the backpack between them. "Sandwich?"

"Of course." Ellie swooped on the wrapped pile of sandwiches and peeled the corner of the bread back. "Yum. Cheese and home-made pickles." She looked up at Hannah. "Another reminder of my grandmother."

"Don't fill up too much. You mightn't enjoy tonight's dinner—and it would be terrible if you couldn't fit in a piece of Mum's lemon meringue pie."

Ellie tipped her head back, squeezed the tips of her fingers together and kissed them. "Don't worry. I would have to be on my deathbed to refuse something like that."

Hannah laughed again. She felt lighter inside—content, even. Her father's oft-used reminder sprang to her mind. *All work and no play makes a person boring.* Was she boring? For six months, she certainly had worked almost every waking hour, and she was weary. Having Ellie here was good for them both.

Satisfied, Hannah dusted the crumbs off her jeans and jumped to her feet. "Come on, girl. We're going shell hunting."

They left their gear tucked into the bank, covered with the towel so the seagulls couldn't ransack their belongings, and headed along the beach to the headland.

It was mid-afternoon before they dragged themselves through the back door and flopped gratefully into the lounge chairs. "Now I know why you're so thin, Hannah. This place is like a health farm—without the massages to help us along."

Hannah threw a cushion at her and chuckled. "Five minutes' rest. Then we'd better get the animals fed if you want a shower before it's time to go to Justin's."

"Slave driver."

Hannah laughed as she walked into her bedroom, but her heart raced a little faster. Soon, she'd be in Justin's home, meeting his mother, eating his food— and staring into those chocolate eyes again.

She swallowed. Here was hoping she could resist his charms once again.

CHAPTER 19

Carol was nothing like what Hannah had imagined. She barely reached her son's shoulder, and her pixie-cut was as white as snow. Her grey eyes matched her cardigan while tight maroon trousers encased her legs. However, it wasn't her clothes or her hair that intrigued Hannah—it was her quiet grace, like a swan sailing calmly over rough water.

Standing on the back porch, she reached up and kissed Dawn and the women held hands, facing each other for what seemed to Hannah like a long time.

"It's been ages," Carol whispered.

Dawn nodded, a smile hovering around her lips. "It has."

Carol turned to Hannah. "And this must be Hannah. I'm delighted to meet you—you look so like your mother." A smile spread over her pale skin.

A moment of shyness gripped Hannah as they exchanged introductions.

"This is my friend, Ellie." Hannah turned toward her while the women shook hands.

Justin waved an arm toward the front of the house. "Go through to the lounge and have a seat. I'll get everyone a drink." Hannah followed Carol and her mother, glancing over her shoulder and meeting Ellie's grin.

In the cosy lounge room, she lowered herself into the unfamiliar chair.

It felt odd. *I'm sitting in our old home and yet nothing is recognisable except the shape and size of the rooms.* She glanced around approvingly. It seemed Justin was not only particular about the lawn and garden, but his organisation and preference for tidiness continued inside, too. Or was that Carol's influence? Apart from a pile of agricultural magazines stacked in a neat pile on the table near the fire, there was no other glimpse of a personal touch—except maybe the picture hanging on the wall? She angled her head to better appreciate it. *Shearing the Rams.* A memento of his years in Aussie? She smiled at the iconic painting by Australian artist Tom Roberts just as Justin entered the room.

"Do you like it?" He glanced toward the picture, and she gave a small nod. "Yes. Can't say I've seen it on too many walls, but I remember being fascinated by the scene when I saw it in book somewhere—high school I think. It really tells a story, doesn't it?"

"Certainly did for me." His gaze swept the room. "What can I get you all to drink?"

While Dawn, Hannah, and Ellie accepted a glass of wine, it surprised Hannah to see Justin offer his mother a lemonade. What was it that Justin had mentioned that day in the woolshed? *Ah yes. His father had been an alcoholic.* Maybe living with him had put Carol off the drink.

Justin excused himself to return to the kitchen and conversation between Dawn and Carol stumbled to a halt. Hannah turned to Ellie and raised her eyebrows, willing her friend to break the silence in her usual effervescent way.

"Mrs Woods, Justin mentioned you help in a dress shop in Hamilton? I love shopping and live in the city. Perhaps it's one I visit." Ellie grinned widely and within seconds, the atmosphere had relaxed as the discussion turned to fashion and shopping.

Hannah twisted her mouth wryly. Retail therapy was certainly not her forte. She glanced down at her jeans and top. Both were clean and ironed—quite adequate in her book. Her thoughts flew to the cocktail dress she'd bought for the evening with Todd that never happened. *Will it hide in the wardrobe until it's out of date and saggy from being on a hanger for so long? Probably.*

The sound of a knife against a chopping board drifted from the kitchen, and Hannah rose to her feet. "I'll give Justin a hand."

She grinned at the trio, deep in conversation, wondering for a second if she should repeat her statement. She shrugged. It didn't matter whether they heard her—so she wandered toward the kitchen.

"Can I help?" she asked. Her nerves jangled.

Justin swung around, a knife poised in his hand. "I reckon I'm all sorted, thanks. You can help me carry this lot out to the veranda, though. I thought we'd have a barbeque and sit out there. It's such a pleasant night."

"Sounds great. I'm not sure I'm game to come any closer though." Hannah pointed to the knife, and he lay it in the sink, grinning. She swept her gaze over the bowls of salads on the table. "You've been busy."

"Not really. Mum did some of them."

His tone was gentle. Was the bond between he and his mother stronger than he'd previously hinted? When he had mentioned her choice of husbands in the woolshed months earlier, Hannah had presumed the relationship between them was more about responsibility than anything else. Perhaps she'd got it wrong?

The evening slipped away in a rush, and Hannah was pleasantly surprised at the speed with which Dawn and Carol appeared to have reconnected after their shaky start.

Ellie laid her spoon on the empty dessert plate and sat back into the cane chair. "Oh, my goodness. That was the best lemon meringue pie I've ever tasted."

The wide veranda provided the perfect spot for dining with the air still and mild. From somewhere close by, a sheep called, its plaintive baa drifting toward the house.

Justin grinned and cast a glance around at the women. "Thanks, Dawn. I agree with Ellie. It's the best I've tasted since ..." He fixed his gaze on Carol. "... Grandma died."

Carol dropped her eyes to the floor, and Hannah froze. Was Carol reluctant to acknowledge her parents? Or was there something else going on here? Her white head lifted, and she stared at Dawn.

"Yes. Thank you, Dawn. I must admit, it was something special that my mother made regularly when Justin and I lived with them."

Dawn reached out and touched her hand. "Do you want to tell us more? You're amongst friends here."

Carol shook her head. "There's nothing to tell. We lived with my parents until Justin was at school—and then I met Nigel." She shrugged, fiddling with the spoon on her empty plate. She gave a small shake of her head. "Anyway, those days are behind us, and we're looking forward to our next chapter, aren't we, Justin?" The edges of Carol's lips lifted, and her expression morphed from one of sadness to hope. Hannah shot her a smile.

"Hannah mentioned you lived out this way many years ago. What made you leave?" Every set of eyes fixed on Ellie, and you could have heard a pin drop in the seconds of silence that followed.

Carol cleared her throat. "It's no secret. My

husband, Justin's father, died. His brothers—and the bank, got the farm, and I moved back to Hamilton to live with my aging parents. End of story."

Hannah looked at Justin, quickly shifting her gaze back to his mother as his eyes met hers.

"Oh," Ellie said and shot Hannah a wide-eyed glance.

Hannah bit her lip. *Hmm, I know what's coming as soon as we leave here.* Ellie was soft and kind—but she loved nothing more than delving into other people's stories.

"Coffee anyone? Tea?" Justin said, and Hannah pushed herself to her feet, eager to break the atmosphere.

"I'll help you."

Justin placed the row of mugs on the kitchen bench while the kettle boiled. "I meant to tell you—I've got a shearing team sorted out so we can get your flock shorn whenever you give the word."

"That's fabulous. Who are they?"

"Two are old mates from the gang I worked with before I went to Australia. Both are still pretty busy, but they said they'd be happy to come up for a change of scenery. One of them has a daughter who's an experienced shed hand, and she'll bring her boyfriend to operate the wool press. They're all honest and it's their livelihood, so you won't have any problems. Anyway, I'll be there to monitor things."

Hannah let the grin spread across her face as her

shoulders slumped. One less worry. "Mum will be pleased, but not as much as I am." She pointed to the row of mugs. "You're a pretty handy coffee maker."

He chuckled and a warmth tingled through her from her head to her toes.

"Would you bring the milk and sugar please? I'll carry the tray of coffees." He handed her a small milk jug and sugar bowl with six teaspoons sticking out of it."

Hannah smiled at the sugar bowl. "Good thing you realise I only have two hands."

He smiled again and inclined his head as he picked up the tray. "Come on. No comments about bachelor habits from you, Ms Simpson."

An hour later, after finishing the evening in a flurry of suds and drying dishes, Hannah stood to leave.

"We're going to visit Ed tomorrow. I thought Ellie might enjoy seeing his garden and meeting our own famous centenarian." She turned to face Justin. "Thanks again. It was a lovely dinner. And thanks for sorting out the shearers for me. The lavender project has preoccupied me." She grinned ruefully. "Never enough hours in the day."

He smiled silently, and Hannah felt an invisible thread of connection between them—something ethereal. Only she wasn't quite ready to strengthen it—not yet.

"It was wonderful seeing you again, Dawn. I plan to return soon—and hopefully we can spend more time together," Carol said, and the two older women hugged. "Thank you for ensuring Justin met Ed as soon as possible. He certainly is a wonderful old man, and I would have been devastated if it had been too late." Carol grimaced.

Hannah blinked back unexpected tears. Her heart ached as the two mothers bid a touching farewell.

"He's quite remarkable and looks twenty years younger than he is. But you're right—none of us know what tomorrow will bring, and in Ed's case, it's even more uncertain than for those of us who have youth on our side." Dawn's smile encompassed them all and Hannah chuckled, her previous wave of emotion gone.

Carol clasped her hands together. "He'll love seeing you all tomorrow. I've promised I'll come and visit at least once a month—provided Justin will have me here, of course."

He moved to his mother's side and lay an arm over her shoulders. "Of course I will." He gave Hannah a cheeky wink. "Looks like I'll be staying around here longer."

Hannah met his gaze and her stomach did a somersault.

———

No one said a word as Hannah drove away from the cottage. They arrived back at the homestead and were filing through the gate before Ellie spoke.

"Did I imagine an underlying reason for Justin's father's death being a no-go subject?"

Dawn sniffed. "It's nearly thirty-five years ago now. He drowned in a lake during duck-shooting season. They deemed it to be an accident ..." She hesitated, squinting as though wracking her brain for further information. "Some people thought it might have been suicide. Others considered foul play."

Ellie hissed. "Wow. Really?"

Dawn continued, hesitantly as they entered the living room. "There was a rumour that he'd had a massive fight the previous night with his brothers. Apparently, neighbours heard raised voices—along with the smashing of glass. Who knows? I remember being more worried about Carol than Ron."

That poor woman. I had no idea.

Hannah screwed up her face. "Justin mentioned something about his uncles not being nice—and his father being an alcoholic? It seems the apple has fallen far from the tree. Or perhaps he really is a genuinely nice bloke?"

Ellie elbowed Hannah in the ribs and giggled. "Well, he certainly couldn't keep his eyes off you tonight."

Hannah snorted and gave her friend a gentle shove. "Don't be ridiculous. We've done a bit of work together, but that's all. He's probably just being polite. Anyway, I've told you already, there's no room in my life for a relationship—and not just because I have too much to do."

Ellie frowned. "Oh, Hannah. Don't let your experience with Todd ruin your chance to love again."

"Who said anything about love?" Hannah snapped. She removed Ragamuffin from the chair and sat down. "You're a good one to talk. When was the last time you had a boyfriend?"

Dawn raised her hands. "I'm off to bed, girls. You two can finish your argument without me."

Hannah swung her glance from her mother back to her friend just in time to catch the guilty, secretive smile that flashed across Ellie's face. Hannah's eyes widened. "You have got a boyfriend."

"I was going to tell you today at the beach … but I didn't want to spoil our time together by filling your head with something that might not even be a 'thing' yet."

"You're a funny one, Ellie. I've spent the last six months holed up here working my butt off and looking forward to some juicy gossip when we finally caught up again—and you kept the most important bit to yourself. Come on, spill!"

Ellie chuckled. "It's early days. His name's Liam, and we met when I went for a walk around Hamilton Gardens a few weeks ago. He's one of the gardeners there." She shrugged. "We haven't been on a date or anything. Just have a talk when I see him—and one day, he shouted me a cup of coffee in the café as it was his break."

"Ah—so it's not actually the gardens that attract you there every weekend."

Ellie yawned. "There's nothing more to tell, and I'm tired. See you in the morning."

Hannah smiled softly as she prepared for bed. It thrilled her that her friend had met someone nice. In their years of acquaintance, Ellie had always shared many details about her stream of boyfriends. The fact that she seemed reluctant to discuss this one spoke volumes.

You deserve a happy relationship, Ellie. I hope something good comes of it.

A twinge of envy filled her as she slid into bed and she gave an enormous sigh.

Maybe one day, someone good would come to her too. Maybe she'd already found him.

CHAPTER 20

The visit to their elderly Norwegian friend was exactly as Hannah had hoped. An instant affinity sprung between Ed and Ellie, and she barely offered a word to their conversation. Listening to others had always been easy for her—especially when they came from the other side of the world and had so many interesting tales to tell.

She bit her lip as Ellie asked about Ed's family and the discussion turned from living in cold northern climes to Hilde. Ed's voice was soft and shaky as he attempted to recall snippets of their childhood.

"It was very different from New Zealand. We were always hungry, always tired. The only wonderful memory I have of the long, cold winters was listening to the stories that our father told—and the songs that our mother sang to us before we went to sleep at night."

Hannah blinked as a vision of Hilde's face rose in front of her. "Sometimes Hilde would sing to me when I was little. I never understood the words, and I didn't like to ask. They seemed so ... so sad?"

Ed laughed. "You're right, Hannah. They were sad—but there wasn't a lot to be happy about for many people. Summer was always my favourite. Berries grew wild in the woods, and Hilde and I roamed the countryside." He paused, dropping his head as though recalling those happy times. "Along with fish, oats, turnips and potatoes, berries were our staple diet in those days."

Ellie screwed up her nose and leaned forward to pick up the plate of baked treats. "Here, Ed. You'd better have another piece of Dawn's chocolate brownie."

A stroll around the garden followed morning tea, and Hannah was astounded by how much Ellie knew about plants. She grinned to herself. Liam?

Amazing what you absorb when you have the right teacher.

———

As she and Dawn said goodbye to Ellie that afternoon, a wave of loneliness washed over Hannah. She was surprised at the sense of emptiness in the house as they stepped back inside—not unlike the void she'd experienced after her father's death.

Hannah glanced at Dawn. Her mother had gone straight to the basket of vegetables she'd dug out of the garden early that morning and began washing them in the sink. *Loneliness must affect her as much as it does me.* A stab of self-pity hit Hannah, and she shook her head slightly. It was her own fault. Dawn kept a tight hold on her habit of calling in to have a cuppa with old friends—and they, in return, frequently popped in to visit her. In contrast, Hannah had focused on the farm and all the responsibilities it entailed.

I'm becoming a hermit. She straightened her shoulders. *No, I'm not a hermit.*

"I'm going to check on the lavender plot. The weed matting should arrive any day now and hopefully the plants will be here this week too."

Dawn smiled. "Of course, dear. It looks as though we're in for a busy few weeks now that the weather is kinder."

Hannah blew out a deep breath as she switched her thoughts to the list of upcoming jobs. "It'll be just our luck to have the plants and the shearers turn up on the same day."

"Well, if that's the case, we'll cope. The plants can sit for a few days while shearing is underway. As long as they get watered regularly, I'm sure they'll be fine."

Hannah wished she had her mother's faith. The nurseryman had reiterated several times the importance of planting out as soon as possible because of the size of the tiny cells that housed the new seedlings. A lump sat at the bottom of her stomach as doubts once more filled her head. *Is this really a good idea? Am I wasting cash on a dream that won't work?*

She whistled at the dogs and strode across the lawn. *This is not the way forward. Get a grip on yourself, girl.*

The rows of brown loam glistened with a soft covering of green.

"Blast. The beds have already been invaded by weeds."

Lass looked quizzically at her, tipping her pretty black and white head from side to side.

Hannah groaned. "Well, I suppose there's only one thing to fix that. I'd better get weeding."

She retraced her steps to the shed and collected the long-handled hoe and a smaller, lighter version with a triangular-shaped head. Determined to keep the lavender organic, she had decided that weed killer would not be an option. She crossed her fingers as she and the dogs returned to the lavender patch. "There's only one way we can do this—and that's plain old hard work!"

She toiled until it was almost dark, perspiration pouring down her back as she uprooted the never-ending weeds. With barely a quarter of the patch cleared, she wiped her sweaty face on her sleeve and arched her back.

The dogs had taken up residence under the tree that grew in the corner of the paddock between the road fence and cattle yards. Hannah grinned at them and lifted her gaze to the setting sun. "Okay. You win. Let's call it a day."

———

FOR THE NEXT TWO DAYS, HANNAH WORKED TIRELESSLY, clearing the weeds from the rows of tilled soil to prepare for the plants. She was both relieved and delighted when she sorted through the pile of mail on Wednesday and saw the envelope with the green circular insignia with a lavender flower inside it. She ripped it open and devoured the contents.

"Hey Mum. The plants and weed matting will be in town, ready to collect tomorrow. Do you want to come with me to get them?"

"Of course I do. We'll need the truck, won't we?"

"Oh. I hadn't thought of that. Perhaps everything will fit in the horse float? I'll ring and find out." She snatched up the delivery advice and raced to the phone in the office.

Minutes later, she returned with a smile plastered on her face. "Yep. He said the weed matting comes in a thick roll but is not long. It should well and truly fit into the float."

"And the plants?" Dawn raised her eyebrows.

"They're in trays which stack on top of one another. All good." She gave her mother a thumbs up sign. "I'll hook the float on now, so we're all ready to head off in the morning. Do you want to give Aunty Jill a ring and see if we can have lunch with her? Make it a day out?"

"That's a lovely idea. You haven't seen them for ages."

Hannah gave Dawn a rueful grin. "I know. While you're doing that, I'll ring Justin and see if he's free to help get the weed mat in place—and ring Uncle George to tell him about our new venture."

She flipped open her mobile and dialled. Once again, the call went unanswered, and Hannah left a message.

Knowing how busy the next couple of weeks would be, she decided to spend the afternoon with the horses, content that Uncle George had received the lavender project information so enthusiastically. *One more brownie point.*

It had been almost seven months since Delight's accident, and Hannah was keen to see how she went under saddle. She ran her hand down the leg. "Looks great. I wish you didn't still limp though. We'll see how we go today and email Kevin tonight with a report."

Dread filled her. Would Delight ever be able to compete again?

She looked around. *Perhaps, more to the point, am I ever going to compete again?*

Within ten minutes of mounting, Hannah's heart sank. There was barely a hint of injury at the walk, but the minute she asked Delight to trot, the uneven gait, the drop of her head, and the anxious flickering of her ears told Hannah what she needed to know. She heaved a sigh and despondently returned to the stables.

She brushed Delight down with long smooth strokes over her gorgeous mare's coat—and an idea came. A foal! She stood back and studied the horse. Except for the leg injury, she was a beautiful mare with good conformation and athleticism. A smile spread over her face and her heart lightened.

Minutes later, she sent a brief email to Kevin, then trawled through the list of friends and acquaintances who shared her passion for show jumping. Eventually, she found what she was looking for—a couple who'd moved from Germany only a year or two before Hannah began competing at an elite level. She dialled their number.

"Of course I remember you," Otto said. "We placed second to you last November in the 1.3 metre class at Woodhill. How are you? I haven't seen you or your mare about lately."

Hannah smiled at the memory. He had ridden a beautiful stallion and had been in first place until Hannah and Delight rode into the ring, the last competitors. He'd been kind when their clear round and quick time pipped his, and his admiration for Delight had been obvious.

Hannah told Otto the tale of Delight's accident and her reasons for returning to Fantail Ridge.

"So, I'm thinking of getting her in foal while she's

too lame to ride. Perhaps if she has a couple of years off, we'll be ready to compete again."

She could hear the man's measured breathing at the end of the phone and waited.

"I'm sorry to hear of both your mare's injury and your father. Please accept my condolences." The line went silent again, and Hannah was about to ask if he was still there when he continued. "Are you looking for a stallion? Or will you choose an imported straw for artificial insemination?"

"Um. I hadn't really got that far. What would you recommend?"

"Let me think about it, Hannah. Would you like to give me your phone number and I will discuss it with my wife and call you back?"

Hannah let her breath hiss out slowly. "Okay. Thank you." She shared her details and hung up just as her computer pinged with an incoming email. She clicked on her inbox icon. "Kevin."

Hey Hannah—good idea. She's got great bloodlines and will be a good broodmare, even if it's temporary. It's hard to tell if she'll ever be sound, but a year or two off will certainly help. Ring me if you've got questions. Kev

Dawn stuck her head around the corner. "Jill's expecting us for lunch. Do you need a hand to get the float on?"

Hannah closed her computer. "Yes please. Two sets of hands—and eyes—are always better than one."

As she walked outside to load the float, her step felt lighter. Perhaps things with Delight could change her future.

We might compete again.

CHAPTER 21

With the plants and matting stowed carefully in the horse float, Hannah turned into the drive leading to her aunt and uncle's home.

Spring bulbs smothered the front paddock, and as she pulled into the turnaround area, Hannah lowered the window, allowing the scent of the blossoms from the plum tree to fill her nostrils.

Jill bounced down the stairs and kissed Dawn on the cheek before throwing her arms around Hannah. Grinning, Hannah rested her chin on her aunt's thick, unruly grey hair, inhaling the familiar fragrance of the fruity shampoo she used.

"It's so good to see you, Hannah. Your mother tells me you've been working much too hard." She gave Hannah a stern look before bursting into laughter and squeezing her again. "I swear, I can even feel your bones."

Hannah grinned and extracted herself from Jill's warmth. "I'm fine. It's good to see spring is here though —with longer days, we'll be able to ramp things up a bit, I hope."

Jill turned toward the house again. "Come on then. Lunch is ready and while we eat, you can tell me all about this new lavender venture of yours. I love the concept."

Barely able to get a word in, Hannah let her aunt chatter on, offering one-word answers while she helped herself to chicken and salad. When Jill stopped speaking, Hannah looked up and met her aunt's blue eyes. Her round face had a healthy, outdoor glow and a kindness that was palpable. One side of her collar was caught in her necklace, and Hannah longed to reach out and straighten it for her.

"And what's this I hear about a good-looking man falling all over you to help?" Jill asked.

Hannah rolled her eyes and looked at her mother. "He's not falling all over me. In fact, he works fewer hours on our farm than he does for most others in the district. Just because he's in my age bracket doesn't mean there's something going on."

"Oh, so you know who I'm talking about then." Jill chuckled.

Hannah huffed. Bloody bush telegraph! "You tell her, Mum."

Dawn shrugged, a soft smile on her face. "He's a very nice young man and the son of an old friend of mine. I have no need to offer anything other than high praise for him. We couldn't have coped these past few months without his help—and this week, he's coming to give a hand getting the lavender planted, and he's organised a shearing team to follow. What's not to like?" Dawn laid her hand over Hannah's. "You're just tired and grumpy and can't see the wood for the trees."

The words exploded from Hannah's mouth before she could stop them. "Mum! From what I've heard, I know several things. His father was violent and an alcoholic. Add to that, I spent four years thinking I was madly in love with a narcissistic and abusive man before I woke up and realised I'm never doing that again. Not exactly the best credentials for a perfect match. The last thing I need is a complication in my life."

"Hannah!" Jill had laid her fork down and was staring at her niece. "You surprise me. You've never been judgemental, and yet here you are, condemning a helpful young man who, from what I can make out from the little I've heard, has done his best to rid himself of his parents' baggage—which he had no control over—and make an honest life for himself. Be fair."

Heat flooded Hannah's neck and crept into her face. "I'm sorry." She collapsed into her chair, her back slumped against the rigid timber, and hid her face in her hands.

Chairs scraped, and kind arms wrapped around her from both sides.

Jill spoke first, her voice soft and kind. "I'm sorry too, Hannah. You've had a rough trot, but it's in the past now, and you've got your whole life ahead of you. Don't let it spoil the person we all know you are."

"It's been a difficult time for you, darling. We understand and are here for you," Dawn finished.

Hannah swallowed her remorse and lifted her head to face them both. "I-I hate admitting it, but I am feeling a bit overwhelmed at the moment."

Dawn snorted. "I noticed." She smiled and shook her head. "You're so like your grandmother. Granny Alice would never say no to anything, even if she was nearly dropping with exhaustion."

Jill had sat down again, and she reached across the table and gripped Hannah's hand. "It sounds like getting this lavender planted is going to be a job that needs as many workers as possible. How about Tim and I come out tomorrow? We'll stay overnight …" She turned to Dawn, who nodded silent approval, "… and we can help."

Hannah blinked back tears of gratitude. "You guys really are the best."

Jill grinned and stood up. "Right then, that's sorted. Now who'd like a piece of apple shortcake and a cuppa?"

———

As good as their word, Jill and Tim arrived minutes after Justin the following morning. The sky was clear, and although cool, the breeze remained gentle.

Hannah and Justin were loading the weed matting, plants, and tools into the carryall tray at the back of Little Red when they arrived. Without waiting, Tim strode toward them and held out his hand to Justin, a grin on his lined, weather-beaten face. Although now in his mid-seventies, Tim remained lithe and fit, surprising even his own family with his ongoing athleticism and quick wit.

Jill followed, zipping up her jacket with a wide grin on her face.

"You must be Justin." Tim waited for Justin's nod. "Great to meet you at last." He turned to Jill. "And this is my wife, Jill."

Justin returned their smiles and wiped his hand on his jeans before extending it. "Sorry about the dirt."

Tim laughed. "Nothing wrong with that." He held out his own work-roughened paw and clasped Justin's.

"Sorry we missed you yesterday, Uncle Tim. Did you win?" Hannah glanced at Justin. "Uncle Tim's a keen golfer. Apparently it never rains on the golf course."

Tim tipped his head back and laughed. "No, sometimes I have to let the others have a little win—otherwise they'd refuse to keep playing with me."

Hannah remembered how much her father had

enjoyed the occasional game of golf with her uncle and her breath hitched. *Why couldn't Dad have had the same good health as you and Uncle George?* The unfairness of it all bit into her.

"Right then. Let's get into it," Tim said. "Who's driving?"

"I will. Little Red's getting touchy these days. Complains a bit about his workload." Hannah snorted.

"Tim, help me carry this food inside please?" Jill asked. "Why don't you go on, Hannah? We'll get this stuff into the fridge and say hello to your mother, then we'll be over."

"Okay. Thanks."

Justin stepped up into the carrier with the equipment and held onto the front of the frame. "Drive on, captain," he quipped. A tingle of anticipation ran through Hannah. Although over a metre separated them, Hannah could almost feel the warmth of his breath on the back of her neck.

———

ROLLING THE WEED MATTING OVER EACH ROW OF HILLED earth took less time than Hannah had expected. Crawling along the edges and pinning it to the ground was much harder, and by the time Jill and Dawn set out morning tea, Hannah had already worn blisters on her hands due to the thin fabric of her gloves.

She glanced over at Justin, his head bowed several

rows over and well ahead of her. He wore a thick glove on his right hand and pushed each pin deep into the ground with barely a pause before moving to the next point.

Her back ached—probably because she hadn't yet recovered from her weeding frenzy, she conceded. Arching, she rubbed the sore muscles and struggled to her feet.

"I'm nipping back to the shed to get a new pair of gloves. You can pour my tea, Mum. I'll only be a few minutes." She gave them all a wave and strode off, Lass and Scruffy bounding along beside her. The ground was soft but dry and the fresh, earthy smell filled her nostrils. A family of magpies warbled as they stared at her from their perch on the roof of the shed. Snatching the brand new pair of leather-palmed gloves from the workbench, she gave a quick glance around. *Have I forgotten anything else? Nope.* She retraced her steps.

From the cattle yards, the land sloped away and a leap of pleasure filled Hannah at the sight of neatly covered rows of dark green weed mat and the group of helpers sitting under the tree in the corner.

Reaching the tree, she smiled at the group. "We might just get it finished today after all."

"I reckon the ladies and I could start planting now, Hannah—if you and Justin are happy to keep going with the pinning down?" Tim asked. "You show us which plants are to be put in and how far apart, and we'll get onto it."

Hannah's heart skipped a beat. This was it. The new project was underway at long last.

"Okay. We've got two different lavender. We'll need to keep each species separate so they don't cross-pollinate. I've marked out a separation area, which I'll plant shrubs in as a dividing line." She reached for a tray of seedlings and squinted at the label. "These are the Angustifolia. They're the ones whose flowers are suitable for culinary recipes like lavender honey and scones. They're also the species that produce less oil, but it's more valuable, so I thought we'd keep them up this end of the paddock, closest to the yards."

She glanced up, a little surprised at the intense stares.

"I'm impressed. What about these?" Justin pointed to the stack of trays on the other side of the tractor's carrier.

"Those are the Intermedia Grosso. Lots of oil and commonly used for perfumes and creams—that sort of thing. We won't be using them for anything edible though, or you'll be complaining about the horrible medicinal aftertaste."

"Right. I'll carry the seedlings if you like, Hannah, and you can show us how you want them planted." Tim lifted a stack of trays and walked down the first row.

While Hannah showed Jill, Dawn and Tim how to snip a hole in the weed mat and plant the seedling, Justin quickly dispensed the balance of the trays before returning to fix each section of fabric firmly to the ground.

The sun beat down on their backs and by lunchtime, they agreed that a two-hour break would be beneficial for all—including the plants.

Hannah had attached a long hose to the tap in the cattle yards and while the older generation returned to the house, she and Justin carted watering cans back and forth to the freshly sown plants.

With the watering complete, they strolled toward the house. An unexplained desire to walk as close to him as possible startled Hannah, and she consciously edged farther away from him, almost missing his comment. *Maybe I have been a bit prejudiced?*

"My mate said they'd be here next Monday if that suits."

Hannah stared at him in confusion. "Your mate?"

"Shearers. The gang I organised to come and shear your sheep—along with myself, of course."

"Oh, sorry. My mind is on the lavender."

He grinned, and she ducked her head. Did he know she was lying?

"When did you say they'd be here? Monday?" Hannah asked as they strolled through the gate.

"Yes. Weather permitting, of course."

"Of course." *Yikes. Today is Thursday already, and it'll be another full day before we've got the lavender planted.* "I'd better get my skates on then." Hannah frowned. "As soon as we finish planting, I'll clean the shed and have the first lot of sheep ready by Sunday night."

"I can help, Hannah. I have nothing booked over the weekend, and I know you've got a lot on your plate at the moment. Let me help—as a friend and not as an employee." She jumped as he touched her arm.

His genuine, caring tone was almost her undoing. She didn't answer for a few moments.

"Thank you. Perhaps on Sunday then? If I get things ready on Saturday, we could bring all the sheep close to the shed and fill the pens ready for Monday. That way, I won't have to be away for as long taking one flock back to the paddock and bringing a fresh lot in."

He smiled as they kicked off their boots. "Good plan."

Her veins fizzed with excited anticipation—and it wasn't only because the list of farm jobs were being ticked off.

CHAPTER 22

They watered the last lavender seedling at three o'clock the following day, and all five adults stood back in admiration. Although the plants were tiny, they appeared strong, and Hannah prayed they would stay that way.

Justin clamped the wire strainers to the fence and tightened each strand. "Nothing will push its way through that," he said as he finished and stepped back to scrutinise his work.

Hannah shot him a thankful smile. "Great, thanks. Actually, I've locked this whole paddock up anyway so we can make hay after Christmas."

She followed his gaze across the rich, green pasture that sloped down to the flat. He nodded and bent down, snapping off a stalk of grass and inspecting it. "Yep. Looks like it was resown fairly recently? It'll make good hay."

"Dad planted it this time last year—and I don't think there's been any stock in it since. I know the paddock is steeper than we usually like for hay-making, but it seems a good way of ensuring no animals will have a hope of pushing through into the lavender."

"Sheep wouldn't eat it, though, would they?"

"I don't think so, but I wouldn't trust them to not trample on the little plants. Best we keep them well clear, at least until they're established and we've had a harvest."

"Good point. By the way, how are the new rams doing? Will there be a paddock full of Dorper-cross lambs bouncing around soon?" He faced Hannah and gave a cheeky wink.

Hannah grinned. "It certainly seems that way. They're good and the ewes are looking pretty heavy. Which reminds me—we'd better leave those rams until last for shearing. I don't want any of that scruffy Dorper wool getting mixed up in the good Romney bales."

Justin saluted. "Aye, aye, captain."

Hannah giggled, and lengthened her stride to match his as they approached the house. They kicked off their boots, washed at the tub in the boot room and stepped into the kitchen. The delicious scent of fresh coffee brewing filled Hannah's nostrils.

"Oh, that smells so good." Justin said, tipping his head back and sniffing.

"We're having a barbeque tonight. Would you like to join us, Justin?" Dawn passed a mug of coffee to each of them and they followed her out to the front veranda. Tim and Jill had each flopped into a cane chair, leaving only the two-seater couch or a stool to sit on.

Hannah moved toward the stool, but she was not quick enough. She almost tripped, sloshing her coffee on the floor as her foot connected with her mother's.

"You two sit on the couch. It's more comfortable, and you've done more than your share of the work," Dawn said with a sly smile.

Hannah shot her mother an annoyed frown and lowered herself onto the couch, taking care to sit as close to the armrest as possible. Justin sat next to her, seemingly oblivious to the electricity in the air. Six inches—she was sure that was the small amount of space between her thigh and his.

"Well, that was a good job completed. Thanks, everyone, for your help." Dawn beamed at Jill and Tim before meeting Justin's grin.

Hannah dragged her attention from the proximity of Justin's muscly, jean-clad leg to the others. "Yes. Thank you all for helping. I know it was my idea and I'm not yet sure if it was a good one, but I appreciate the support and help you've all given me."

Tim leaned forward, his half-empty mug clasped in both hands. "So what happens next, Hannah? You mentioned distilling the oil. How do you do that?"

Hannah groaned. "That's the next worry. I've spent

hours trawling through the internet trying to find what we need but haven't had any luck so far. There seems to be a million different types of stills for alcohol and much bigger plantations like they use in Europe, but nothing that will fit the bill for our little set-up."

"So what exactly do you need?" Tim finished his coffee and placed his mug on the side table.

"I need something that will produce steam, just like for whiskey. It has to be able to move through the lavender flowers consistently and without congestion." Hannah absorbed the interested stares on both Justin's and Tim's faces. "I've spoken to a bloke in Australia who used one he had specially made. It has a bag about the size of a bed-roll that holds a wheelbarrow-load of lavender flowers at a time. An old-fashioned steam generator sucks water from a tank and converts it to steam, which then blows through the bag of flowers. The oil-laden steam rises and is forced through a condenser which has cold water piped through an inner tube, cooling the contents. It separates them and the hydrosol—or lavender water—flows one way and the oil the other. Because of the sealed system, the water is recycled, so it doesn't even use ridiculous amounts of H_2O. Sounds easy, doesn't it?"

Dawn nodded while Jill stared at Hannah with a look of total confusion on her face.

Tim clasped his fingers together and rotated his thumbs around each other. "I think we could probably make something suitable. We've got that old steam generator Mum and Dad used yonks ago in the shed at home. I reckon with a bit of TLC, we could get it operational again."

"Really?" Hannah gaped at Tim. "That's fabulous."

"I'd like to help—if you don't mind?" Justin said. "Science was my favourite subject at school, and one of my projects was making a miniature still in class. I reckon we could nut something out together—especially as I've already had a chat with Ed, and we've sketched out a few designs."

Hannah stared at him in surprise. "You kept that quiet."

He shrugged, and Tim beamed at him. "You're on."

Dawn rose to her feet. "Well, that's one issue sorted. Now it's time I prepared a couple of salads for tea. Tim, would you uncover the barbeque please and make sure there're no spiders or mice in residence?" She glanced at Hannah and grimaced. "It's a while since we used it last, 'ey Han?"

Hannah nodded. "I'll feed the animals and lock up the chooks. Be back shortly." She hurried into the kitchen, grabbed the chook bucket, and darted off without a backward glance. At the fowl run, she threw the scraps on the ground, while the hens scratched and squabbled amongst themselves.

Humiliation at her outburst at Jill's house earlier in the week still rankled. Was she making excuses? She found Justin incredibly attractive. It was just ... well, she had agreed with herself that she would note the negative side of people instead of always seeing the best in them and ignoring red flags. "I don't trust myself. That's my problem."

"Oh, really? In what way?"

She spun around, mortified. Justin. "Oh, um—it's nothing. I was thinking about the decisions I've made on the farm since Dad died."

Justin stepped closer to her and smiled softly. "Hannah, you're doing a fantastic job, and from what I can see, I don't think your mum would have coped without you. Stop punishing yourself for stuff you have no control over."

"You're a fine one to talk. Didn't you say you're not interested in having a relationship with anyone because of your family history?" She clapped her hand over her mouth, surprised at her outburst.

Justin stared at her for what seemed like ages before his shoulders slumped. "You're right. I did." He stepped through the henhouse door, standing less than a metre away, his head almost touching the wire netting above them. "Only I didn't bargain on meeting such a beautiful and capable woman who would wreck my ability to sleep properly."

Hannah dropped her gaze and scuffed a boot in the dirt. Sucking in a quick breath, she raised her head again, just as Justin bent and kissed her. A warm flood of relief filled her as his arms wrapped around her. She dropped the empty bucket and tentatively reached up to curl her hand around his neck. Their kiss deepened, and she clung to him with a deepening passion—one she had never experienced.

A dog barked, and she jumped back, touching her lips with her fingers. "Oh."

"Oh?" He smiled. "I hope that's a good 'oh'?"

She nodded. "I think it might be."

Lass leaped around their feet, and she looked down and smiled. "They're reminding me why I'm here—to feed them."

Justin bent and picked up the empty scrap bucket. "I'll help."

Hannah latched the gate shut behind them and turned back to his outstretched hand. She hesitated, her hand poised in mid-air. *What am I doing?* And then she took it and they walked toward the dog kennels.

———

IT WAS A LONG TIME BEFORE HANNAH COULD SLEEP THAT night. She tossed and turned, worrying about getting tangled up in a relationship that might be wrong for them both. Their mothers were friends. Was that not a good reason to maintain separation? What if something happened to their friendship? Would that then drive Justin and Hannah apart? And what about the farm? It was hers and her mother's. Did Justin think he could take it over? She'd read about couples having to go to court when a property was owned by one and the other claimed rights to it after being in a relationship for a few years.

Then his face appeared in her mind and she smiled into the dark. She was being ridiculous. Aunty Jill was right. She wasn't allowing either of them a chance at happiness—and who knew what the future would bring, anyway? Look at her dad, and so many friends and acquaintances who had lost their lives way too early.

She rolled over and fell into a deep, dreamless sleep.

———

HANNAH SPENT ALL OF SATURDAY PREPARING THE woolshed for shearing. She scrubbed the boards until all traces of grease and manure were minimised, before wiping the cloudy, fly-spotted windows. Then she dusted and de-cobwebbed the grinder and shearing plant in readiness for a busy few days.

Her heart leapt when the sound of Justin's ute drew close on Sunday morning. Even the horses sensed her excitement and Cruiser swung his hindquarters from side to side, dancing as she led them out of the stables.

With ears pricked, they too seemed to welcome Justin as he stepped out of the vehicle and hurried to the passenger-side door. Hannah's eyes widened as Carol emerged.

"Hello!" Hannah called, trying to keep the surprise from her voice.

"Hi." He strode over to Hannah, hesitated for a moment, then kissed her softly on the cheek. "Hope you don't mind. Mum turned up last night for a few days. She says she's helping your mother cook for the shearers."

Monty nudged him, and they both laughed.

Hannah handed Justin Monty's reins and mounted Cruiser. "That's great. Mum will be delighted."

Carol was already strolling toward the house, and Hannah called after her. "Hi Carol. Mum's in the kitchen. Just give her a cooee—she'll be pleased to see you."

Carol waved, and the gate closed behind her.

Hannah glanced down at Jet and Lass, sitting patiently and waiting for instructions. "Great welcoming party you two are. You didn't even say hello to Carol."

Justin strapped on his helmet and grinned at her. "Looks like they know they've got a far more important job to do today." He put his foot in the stirrup and swung his leg over the saddle. "Okay, partner. Let's do it."

With both horses and dogs fresh and eager, it took less than an hour to reach the back of the farm. They worked along the fence line, pushing the sheep toward the open gate at the foot of the hill. The flock moved as one—a thick cloud of cream racing down the slope and funnelling through the gap onto the formed track that led homeward.

Slowing to a walk, Hannah called to Justin, "I'll keep them moving if you can close the gate, please?"

He waved in acknowledgement, and Hannah smiled. Her heart was bursting. As she passed a clump of native bush, a fantail emerged, twittering overhead and flitting back and forth, catching insects disturbed by the musterers. She glanced over her shoulder and smiled as Justin urged Monty into a canter to catch up with her.

"We've got company." She pointed at the fantail. "Aren't they the cutest little birds?"

Justin grinned and nodded. "My favourites are the wrens. So tiny and yet so efficient and beautiful."

A ewe paused in front of them, snatching at a mouthful of grass from the side of the track, and Jet let out a loud bark.

The sheep leapt forward, joining the flock and startling its neighbours. Breaking into a run, the mob followed, and Hannah whistled for Lass. The collie began traversing the leaders, containing them in a tight bunch and slowing the pace.

By midday, more than half of the Fantail Ridge flock were in the yards and network of small paddocks surrounding the woolshed.

"Let's have some lunch before we bring the rest closer," Hannah said as she closed the gate behind them. She dismounted and patted both dogs, ruffling their ears and making a fuss of them. "Good job, you two."

The dogs waited until she swung her arm forward and then jumped into the trough at the edge of the big holding yard, their tongues lolling and their sides heaving.

Jet leapt out of the water first, shaking himself violently and showering everything within the surrounding few metres, including Hannah. She looked down at her damp-spotted shirt and laughed. "Good on you, Jet. I needed that—not!"

Justin grinned at her. He'd quickly jumped away and avoided the unwanted shower. "Shall we take the horses back to the house or leave them here?"

"Take them home. That sun is getting warm and the sheep are using all the shade." She raised her eyebrows and dragged the reins over Cruiser's head.

Walking hand in hand, Justin and Hannah led the horses to the stables, unsaddled them, and left them chewing hay. A comfortable peace settled over Hannah —a feeling she had forgotten was possible. She squeezed Justin's hand and met his smile.

As they walked, the scent of lavender and hay mingled in the air, and Hannah's heart sung. *This is what promise smells like.*

CHAPTER 23

Shearing went without a hitch, with only a brief shower of rain in the early afternoon on Tuesday.

While Justin and his friends worked tirelessly in the shed, the bales of pressed wool piled up beside the sliding door of the landing dock. Dawn and Carol arrived at two-hourly intervals, laden with fresh sandwiches, sausage rolls, scones, cakes, fruit—and a smorgasbord of cold meat and salads for lunch.

Hannah released a sigh of happiness. Sitting outside, her shoulders pressed against the corrugated-iron wall. She took a bite of a piece of ginger crunch and turned her face to the cooling breeze. The rest of the shearing gang were lounging inside the woolshed, one man flat on his back while the others rested against packed wool bales.

"Everything okay outside, boss?" Justin lowered himself down beside her, his elbow briefly touching hers. It eased her mind that he kept any hint of their budding relationship from the rest of the gang. Gossip spread quickly, and it was too early yet even for her to comprehend what was happening between them.

"All good. I took the mob we brought in on Sunday back to the paddock next to Hosking's deer fence. It's warm and will keep the ewes in good order before they lamb."

The farm next to Fantail Ridge's western boundary had recently become a thriving deer facility, and high mesh fences now ran the length of every one of their neighbours' paddocks. Hannah was happy about the situation. Bill Hosking had worked with her father to ensure a row of trees filled the gap between the new fence line and their own wire and batten surroundings. It was a win-win for all, offering the Fantail Ridge stock additional protection from the strong westerly winds.

"How many left to shear?" Justin asked.

"We're down to the last five hundred. Hopefully, the weather will stay like this until we're finished." Hannah flicked crumbs off her jeans and bit into an apple. "If you guys get them done by lunchtime tomorrow, there'll only be the rams to shear. I've got the two Dorper boys in the back pen already, and I'll bring the Romneys over from Granny's park in the morning."

Justin nodded, a smile of admiration spreading across his face. "There's no doubt about it, Hannah. You're a good organiser."

She huffed. "Sometimes." Her thoughts flew to the promotion she'd failed to win at the research station. "Apparently not everyone thinks so."

He said nothing—but to Hannah, the warm sympathy shining from his beautiful brown eyes said it all.

———

WITH THE SHEARING BEHIND THEM AND A FEW WEEKS before lambing would begin, Hannah spent most days working in the lavender patch. As the weather warmed and showers scudded across the land, the extent of work involved in keeping unwanted growth from creeping over the edges of the weed mat surprised Hannah. Determined not to weaken and use chemicals, she chipped the offending greenery daily, convincing herself that a regular stroll up and down each row was beneficial anyway. All the tiny plants had taken quickly and were thriving in the well-drained soil, and the Intermedia plants were already double the size of the Angustifolia.

She had seen little of Justin over the past couple of weeks as it seemed everyone else in the district was also clamouring for his help. She didn't mind the space between them; it gave her time to think, to weigh up her feelings, and to look back at her past mistakes. She'd known from the outset that Todd was a ladies man—a real charmer. She'd succumbed to his flirtatious compliments herself and ignored the excessive drinking and quick temper. Within a year of dating, she had known it wouldn't work—and been too blind and naïve to admit it.

Warm from both the sun and thoughts of Justin, Hannah returned to the homestead to join her mother for lunch one day in late October, surprised to see Dawn dressed in her 'going to town' clothes.

"I didn't realise you were going out?" she asked.

"I wasn't—however, Ed rang an hour ago and asked if I would take him in to see the solicitor. Evidently, he's let the Radleys buy him out now on the proviso they allow him to stay in the house as long as he needs to. They've agreed and have had documents drawn up, so he's keen to sign everything."

"Oh?" Hannah frowned. "Is that wise? I mean, they wouldn't chuck him out or anything, would they?"

Dawn shook her head. "Of course not. You know June Radley. You couldn't find a kinder person. No, I think it's more that Ed seems to have realised he will not be here forever and it will make life easier for everyone if he gets 'all his ducks in a row', so to speak, sooner rather than later."

Hannah nodded. "I suppose so. I just hate to think of the poor old man being taken advantage of."

Dawn rested a hand on Hannah's arm. "Of course, love. He's very special to us all. But that's why we need to get the legal documents in place—to protect him in every way possible."

"Fair enough. I'll have a quick bite to eat, then shift the heifers into a fresh paddock. Shouldn't be long, so don't worry about dinner. I'll cook."

Dawn smiled at her daughter. "Thanks, dear. See you later." Then she picked up her handbag and hurried out the door.

Hannah was eating slowly, flicking through the latest horse magazine, when the phone rang. She put the half-eaten sandwich back on the plate and trod the few paces to the office desk.

"Hello, Hannah speaking."

"Hello Hannah. It's Otto. I'm sorry it has taken me so long to get back to you."

Hannah's eyes widened. It had been a while. However, she acknowledged, he had as busy a life as she did.

"Lovely to hear from you, Otto. Please don't apologise. I know how busy life gets." She paused, her stomach fluttering with anticipation.

"I have discussed your mare with my wife, Marie, and we have two suggestions to offer you. We have some imported semen straws from a German stallion that has progeny achieving at a high level in Europe." He continued with the details of bloodlines and accolades, and Hannah's head spun, uncertain where the information was leading. "We're prepared to offer you one straw for your mare if you would like it."

"H-how much would it cost?"

Otto named an eye-watering price, and Hannah

slumped into the chair. "Oh. I'm sorry, Otto. I really couldn't afford that amount."

"We thought that may be the case but wanted to make the offer, anyway. The other option is for you to bring Delight to us for a couple of weeks and we will monitor her until she cycles, then join her with Pilot, our stallion. As you know, he's a gentle boy and easy to handle. I think he would suit both you and your mare, and together, they would make a nice foal without costing you too much."

Hope warmed Hannah, and she sat up straight. It sounded too good to be true. "Um. What would the fees be?"

He named a stud fee that was within Hannah's budget, and a far more reasonable agistment cost than she had expected.

"Perhaps you could bring her to us soon—that way you would hopefully have a nice foal on the ground before Christmas next year."

Excitement bubbled in Hannah, her pulse racing. "That would be wonderful. Thank you. Are you still living near Cambridge?" *I could visit Ellie at the same time.*

"No. We moved to a farm near Kaukapakapa a year ago. More land and still convenient enough to attend competitions and shows."

Hannah blinked. *So close.* "Fabulous. I am close to Helensville, so we can be to you in an hour. When would it suit to bring her over?"

"Whenever suits you, Hannah."

"Tomorrow?" She clutched the desk in anticipation.

He chuckled. "That would be fine. I'll email you a copy of both our procedure and contract." He detailed how to get to the property, and Hannah scribbled the instructions down before finishing the call.

She looked at Scruffy, lying in his basket on his back, feet in the air, while the sun streamed through the open window. "What do you think of that, little dog? We've found a husband for Delight, and she can have a baby!" She crossed her fingers in both hands and held them up, her smile widening.

After quickly finishing the remnants of her lunch, Hannah hurried to the paddock and caught Delight.

"I think we'd better give you a wash and polish." Hannah rubbed away the crusts of mud clinging to Delight's mane and gave her a rueful grin. "Come on. Bath time."

For the next hour, Hannah scrubbed the horse, rinsed her off, and combed out her mane and tail. She sorted through the pile of rugs and picked out a clean rip-stop cover and matching neck rug. Then she trimmed her hooves before leading her into a clean stable and filling the hay net.

"Tomorrow morning, we're taking you to meet your prince charming—but now, I need to shift the heifers." She chortled, letting anticipation and a ray of optimism fill her heart.

———

IT WAS ALMOST DARK BY THE TIME DAWN ARRIVED HOME, tired but resolute.

"That was a tough call. Poor Ed. I wonder if he hasn't been feeling as well as usual lately. He's obviously been giving a lot of thought to both his past life and how he wants to be remembered."

"Oh. Like what?" Hannah dished up a piece of smoked fish with parsley sauce for each of them before spooning out the freshly dug potatoes and a mix of steamed vegetables from the garden.

"Well, it wasn't only the documents relating to the sale of his farm we went through with the solicitor. There was his will and all the details about where he wants to be buried and what he wants to happen at his service."

"Oh, Lord. That would have been a bit confronting. Sorry, Mum. I should have gone with you." Hannah lay a protective hand on her mother's arm.

Dawn shook her head. "I was fine. I must admit, though, I'd forgotten they listed your father and me as both his enduring power of attorney and the executors of his will. That's now Hugh Bennett and I."

"Is Hugh happy about that?"

"Yes. Both Ed and the solicitor had spoken with him, and he agreed. After all, Hugh's known Ed all his life. He even remembers Ed giving him rowing lessons in their dinghy when he was a tiny child. Hugh's a good, fair man, and I'm sure he and I will be able to ensure Ed's wishes are followed."

Hannah gave a small nod. "Good. Now I've got something to tell you."

Dawn's gaze lifted from the meal Hannah laid in front of her. "Sounds exciting. Tell."

"I'm taking Delight to Otto and Marie Muller's place tomorrow. You remember—the German couple parked next to us last year at the Woodhill comp. They had that lovely big bay stallion and were miffed when Delight and I beat them in the metre-thirty class."

Dawn grinned. "Oh yes, I remember them." A look of confusion flashed across her face. "But why?"

"To get in foal to him. Pilot, their stallion."

Dawn lay her cutlery down and clapped her hands. "Oh, how wonderful! What a good idea."

Hannah chuckled. "I didn't tell you about it earlier because I wasn't sure if it would be possible."

Dawn covered Hannah's hand with her own. "Of course. I know how much that poor head is trying to process at the moment. I understand."

Under her mother's soft, loving gaze, Hannah's lip quivered. She picked up her cutlery and began eating.

She just hoped she could keep on juggling it all—and that she didn't break.

CHAPTER 24

Slowing almost to a halt at the entry gates, Hannah gasped. Huge stone walls flanked either side of the gateway, signalling opulence, while a large, carved timber sign confirmed she was in the right place. *Winterbern Stud—O & M Muller.*

"This is it." She crawled the car down the driveway lined with poplar trees and white-painted fences. A huge brick home sprawled across the top of the gentle rise in front of her, and to one side at the rear, she glimpsed a long, low stable block. The driveway split in two with a signpost at the divide, surrounded by standard yellow roses.

Following the sign to the stables, Hannah continued on, her eyes widening as she approached a massive indoor arena. In the centre of a flat area, encircled by more stables, appeared to be staff quarters and a veterinary centre. *Wow. This is amazing.*

She parked in the designated area and made her way to the small door at the front of the horse float. "Cripes, Delight. You've come to the Taj Mahal! I suggest you enjoy it."

Delight flicked her head up and down, and Hannah grinned as she released the lead rope from the tie ring.

Footsteps on the gravel outside drew close, and Hannah backed her way out of the float.

"Hello. You must be Hannah." The slim, elegant woman in cream breeches, long black boots, and a bright pink polo shirt held out her hand. "I'm Marie."

Hannah smiled and shook it, a little surprised to be greeted by the owner and not a stable-hand after what she had already seen. Caught in a knot at the base of her neck, Marie's blonde hair gave her a casual appearance and yet somehow, she still exuded class.

"Otto's coming. We have finished our morning program and are about to have coffee. Would you like to unload your horse? We can help you get her settled, then we can all have a drink together." Her voice held only the slightest hint of an accent, and beside her, Hannah felt a little like the country cousin.

She glanced down at her clean jeans and white shirt smothered with tiny forget-me-knots. It was her favourite, and she had thought it smart—until now. "Thank you very much. That would be lovely."

She released the bolts on the tail ramp and lowered it to the ground before unclipping the bum bar.

"Back up, girl." Hannah made a clicking sound and

Delight took a backward step, easing herself out of the float. Grabbing the trailing lead rope, Hannah let the mare stand for a minute and gaze around. Delight seemed as impressed as her owner, standing tall and flicking her ears. She gave a long, loud whinny, and both Marie and Hannah smiled.

"Welcome to you too, Afternoon Delight." Marie turned toward the stables and beckoned Hannah to follow.

They approached a series of large loose boxes surrounding a grass-covered quadrangle.

"This is where we keep the mares for breeding. It means they're handy to monitor for oestrus." She indicated the steel vetting crush at one end, complete with a wide shelf containing an array of scanning equipment, a computer screen, and an assortment of gloves and pharmaceutical items.

Wow. This is way more than a simple horse stud—it's serious business. Hannah had understood her precious horse would not wander at will with the stallion in a safe and lush paddock—but the set-up in front of her was far superior to what she'd imagined as the alternative.

"You have your own veterinary facility, I see?" Hannah asked.

Marie nodded. "I am a qualified veterinarian—but I don't practice except in our own business." She held a finger to her lips. "I love the horses but am not really interested in tending to other animals, so I keep up my registrations but don't advertise my qualifications."

"Oh." Hannah didn't know what to say. *I love animals. I couldn't imagine feeling that way.* Instead, she walked beside Marie to a loose box, released Delight and gave her a reassuring pat. Then she followed her hostess to the wide house veranda overlooking the farm.

"Have a seat." Marie indicated the wicker chairs filled with colourful cushions that surrounded a glass-topped table. "I'll bring the coffee out." And she disappeared into the cavernous living area of the home.

An hour later, with forms completed, a signed cheque handed over, and still savouring the flavour of rich coffee and tiny almond biscuits, Hannah drove back down the drive and onto the road home.

I hope it all happens quickly and pleasantly for you, Delight. The friendliness of both Marie and Otto and their attention to safety and detail had softened her opinion of them. Reassured Delight was in expert hands, Hannah accelerated and turned her mind to the chores waiting for her at home.

———

HANNAH'S EYES WIDENED AS SHE DROVE INTO THE YARD. Both Tim's and Justin's vehicles sat in front of the shed, the men standing under the awning's shade, facing her. She turned the engine off and left her car and float where they were, her smile growing as she approached them.

"I didn't expect you two here today. What's happening?" she asked.

Tim pushed his hat back and scratched his thick, grey hair, meeting her smile with a wide grin. "Come and see."

She raised her eyebrows at Justin and followed Tim into the shed.

Next to the long, scrubbed table that Hannah had prepared for bunching the harvested lavender was a stainless-steel contraption with a large bag attachment. Copper tubes led from the main bowl to a second container and several pieces of pipe and smaller vessels lay on the table beside it.

Hannah clapped her hands. "The still!" She stared at Justin before swinging her gaze to her uncle. "How did you get this? Did you make it?"

"Settle down, Han. Yep, this young fella and I nutted out a bit of a design, and I talked it over with a bloke I used to work with at the dairy factory. We came up with a drawing, and this is the prototype." Tim rubbed his chin and gazed at them both. "So, what do you reckon?"

Hannah drew a long breath, her shoulders raised in excitement. "I guess the proof of the pudding is in the eating, as they say. Does it work?"

Tim laughed while Justin shrugged.

"We hope so. Spent enough time on it. You need to

provide us with the lavender now, and we'll give it a run," Tim replied.

"Hmm. You might have to wait another few weeks for that. They're not even budding yet." She met Justin's gaze and returned his gentle smile. It had been weeks since she'd seen him and had presumed it was shearing that was keeping him busy—but apparently not.

"Your mum said you'd taken Delight to a stallion somewhere. How did you get on?" Justin asked.

Hannah nodded at Justin and held up crossed fingers. "Well, if Otto and Marie's set-up is anything to go by, I'd say we're off to a good start. It's not only a stud but also a fully equipped riding facility, breeding farm, and veterinary centre."

"That sounds perfect," Tim said.

Hannah grimaced. *Yes, this is only the beginning.*

Tim walked toward the little house gate and Justin brushed a kiss on her cheek. "Your mum invited me for lunch," he whispered.

Hannah beamed at him, pausing. "Good. It feels as though it's been years since I saw you last." She glanced at her uncle's retreating figure as Justin wrapped her in his arms and hugged her tight, wiping away all thoughts except those of the man beside her.

———

OVER LUNCH, THE CONVERSATION TURNED TO THE upcoming lambing, due to begin the following week.

"The ewes that you put to the Dorper rams look as though they're about to drop any day." Justin passed the salad bowl to Hannah, his eyes filled with concern. "I suspect there'll be a lot of multiple births so you may end up with a few to bottle-rear."

Hannah shrugged. "That's okay. We do most years, so Mum's used to it—and so was I before I left home. Only difference is that now we don't milk a cow, we have to ensure we've got plenty of milk-powder handy."

"I've taken on a contract to help those new people farther out on the peninsula set up their deer farm." Justin speared the cold meat on his plate, smothering it with chutney before lifting his gaze to Hannah. "Seeing as that flock are in the paddock below the cottage, I could have a quick walk around them each morning before I leave if you like …? Give you the heads up if I think anything's not quite right?"

"Thanks, Justin. That would be fabulous. I'll start a daily lambing beat as soon as the first lamb is on the ground. For the moment, though, keeping the lavender free of weeds seems to take priority." Hannah rolled her eyes.

Dawn rose to pour the tea and handed the mugs around the table. "I've been talking to your mother, Justin."

Both Hannah and Justin simultaneously stared at her.

"Don't look at me like that." Dawn laughed. "Carol

and I were friends long before you two came along, and it's been lovely to get reacquainted. She rings me one week and I return the call the following." She pursed her lips. "Anyway, I was about to tell you we've been discussing the lavender."

Hannah laid her cutlery down. "And?"

"We can both sew—and enjoy it. So ... we thought perhaps we could help by making lavender bags and heat bags—you know, stuff like that. Carol said she's got a recipe for soap-making too, so is keen to have a try with that once there's some lavender oil available."

Hannah's interest grew. "I spoke to the lady in the gift shop in town and she said she'd be happy to sell our products on consignment. I wonder what else we can do?"

"Carol is happy to try the dress shop where she works—perhaps displaying a basketful of your wares on the counter. That sort of thing. I'm sure we'll think of other options—I just wanted you to know that we're here for you, Hannah, and are keen to help."

Hannah gulped her tea, the warmth flowing through her veins—and not only from the hot drink. She was surrounded by those she loved most, and their support urged her on.

She had never been happier.

CHAPTER 25

Days later, lambing began in earnest. The air was filled with high-pitched bleats of newborns, reciprocated by the deep, reassuring baaing of their mothers. Every turn Hannah made, another ewe was struggling to deliver, and, just like riding a bike, she was relieved her skills as a sheep midwife had not been forgotten.

"I don't know why some years we have no trouble, and others we seem to have more lambs on the bottle than in the paddock," Dawn said, shrugging as Hannah apologetically handed her another abandoned lamb. "Well, slight exaggeration, but you know what I mean."

Hannah frowned. "I thought we'd be fine this season, especially as we did a pretty thorough selection process."

"Don't worry, dear. We haven't got nearly as many maiden ewes as we've had some years. It's all part of the gamble in farming. This is obviously one of those seasons." Dawn cuddled the lamb against her and rubbed her cheek on the top of its head.

Hannah certainly hoped so. Her exhausting rides around the sheep each day, catching ewes in difficulty, delivering lambs, and bringing home any that appeared abandoned were taking a toll on her. Cruiser, however, took it all in his stride, showing remarkable patience. He appeared to realise the importance of his cargo and trod steadily home with barely a flick of his ears—aside from one initial snort when Hannah laid the lamb sling behind the saddle. The hessian carrier had a pocket on either side and was large enough to carry up to three newborn lambs on each side. The gentle gelding took his job seriously.

"This is better than galloping in endless circles, isn't it, mate?" Hannah chuckled and Cruiser turned his head to the side, checking his load before he walked forward. Tied to the D-rings on the front of her saddle, the medical bag contained a bottle of injectable antibiotic, needles and syringes, medical gloves, and other appropriate supplies.

Frequently, Hannah had tied a sheep against a fence while holding a lamb against the ewe's udder, willing the mother to accept her offspring. When all else failed, she milked colostrum from the ewe and hand-fed the lamb. Then, after releasing the ewe back into the flock, she took the newborn home to add to the growing creche. The lambs were divided between a heated box in the boot room, a hay-filled pen in the shed, and the orphan enclosure in the paddock beside the chook pen. The daily chore of feeding each age group by hand up to six or seven times a day remained a joy for Dawn, even after thirty years. For that, Hannah was grateful.

Eventually, the six weeks of births ended, and both women breathed a sigh of relief. On the plus side, they had more multiple births than ever before, including four sets of triplets and hundreds of twins. The flip side meant the milk powder and lamb muesli needed, pushed the feed bill to an alarming height. Hannah was confident it was money well spent. *At least we've had very few losses this year.* She glanced up at the sky. *I think you'd approve, Dad.*

———

HANNAH THREW OPEN THE KITCHEN DOOR AND CALLED out, "The lavender's in bud!"

Dawn hurried from the depths of the living room, her slippers scuffing across the lino floor. "Wonderful. So—do we start cutting?"

"Not sure. Come and see what you think?" Hannah could barely stop herself from jumping up and down on the spot while she waited for her mother to shove her feet into old shoes. They made their way out to the lavender field.

December had arrived—the long days stretching into balmy evenings and the signs of healthy growth were everywhere.

With the strain of lambing season now over, Hannah threw her time and energy into the lavender, horrified at the number of weeds that had encroached on the crop. Despite the competition, the plants had grown well, and anticipation buzzed through Hannah's veins.

She and Dawn bent over the rows, inspecting the fresh growth and early flowers.

Hannah straightened. "I think it's time we started harvesting? What do you think?" A grin spread across her face.

"I agree. Let's begin."

She hauled out the shallow baskets, garden snips, knee pads and gloves she'd purchased in readiness and handed one of each to her mother.

"We'll work our way through one species at a time so we don't get them mixed up." Doubt suddenly filled Hannah as she realised the enormity of the project. This was a job that required a team of pickers—not just a woman in her sixties and her optimistic daughter.

Dawn nodded. "Right. Let's get to it. If the weather stays this warm, those buds are going to open quickly and from what you've told me, we need to get them tied in bunches and hanging in the drying cupboard as soon as possible."

The weather held and each morning, the two women crawled along the rows before taking the flowers back to the shed to prepare them for the drying process.

By the end of the week, Hannah's anxiety had escalated. Not only was the lavender producing more buds and flowers than she had expected this early in the season, but the hundreds of growing lambs in the paddock had still not been ear-tagged or castrated.

While stewing over how she should manage the workload, Jill called.

"How's it all going?" Jill asked.

Hannah groaned. "Well—but I think the lavender believes we're in a race. Mum and I are struggling to keep up." She chuckled to lighten her concerns. "Plus, we haven't had time to get the new lambs sorted." She let out a long breath while the line remained silent for a few seconds.

"We'll come and spend a few days with you—if you can put up with us. Tim can stay away from the golf course and put his energy into helping you with the sheep. It'll do him good."

Hannah smiled at her aunt's determined tone. *I'm not sure that Uncle Tim would agree with you.*

After clarifying a few details, Hannah hung up and hovered by the phone for a few seconds. Should she ring Justin and ask him to help too? His fencing contract was a big one. If she admitted she was struggling to cope, she was sure he would want to drop everything and come to her aid—and that may put him in a difficult situation for ongoing work with other farmers. In the end, she decided they would cope without him.

She returned to the shed where Dawn was tying the flowers in little bunches and shared the news of her aunt's offer.

"Thank goodness for Jill. She really is a trojan—and I think they enjoy coming out, anyway. During all those years when Tim worked long hours, and you kids were growing up, we didn't get as much time together as I would have liked. It'll be nice to have them here." Dawn gathered up an armful of bunches and placed them in the basket.

Hannah agreed with a silent smile and picked up the laden basket of flowers and buds. "Let's get these into the drying cupboard and clean the table so we can start on the Angustifolia in the morning."

Hannah headed inside and switched on the hall light, her mother trailing after her, carrying a second basketful. They halted beside the row of ceiling-height cupboards.

"Granny certainly believed in plenty of storage," Hannah said. She flung open the doors of two cavernous storage areas, cleared in readiness for their new life as drying cupboards.

Hidden inside the end closet beside the bathroom, the hot water cylinder sent a gentle flow of warmth through the adjoining areas. Having been used for linen, spare bedding, Christmas decorations, and many other odd items over the years, each cubicle was filled with slatted shelves, offering the perfect hanging facility for hundreds of lavender posies. After stringing them on rows of wire, Hannah attached the ends to the undersides of each rack, allowing the flowers to dry upside down in the dark. She hoped two weeks would be sufficient. Until then, they would remain suspended above a paper-covered shelf to catch any seeds that fell.

On the outside of each door, she taped a simple sign showing which cupboard held which species of lavender.

While Hannah strung the last row, Dawn retreated to the bathroom to wash her hands. Hannah closed the cupboard, a satisfied smile on her face at the exact moment the phone rang. Situated a metre away from where she stood, the loud ringing, designed to be heard if the occupants were outside, made Hannah jump.

She snatched up the handpiece. "Hello?"

"Hannah. It's George. How are you?"

Her heart sank. Uncle George rarely rang unless there was a financial issue he wanted to discuss, or he felt the need to share a dose of wisdom or opinion with his sister-in-law and niece. "We're well. And you?"

"Good thanks. What are you doing at the moment?"

Hannah frowned. Where was this going? "We're busy with the start of the lavender harvest and are hoping to get the lambs docked and tagged in the next week, too. So … we've got plenty to keep us out of trouble." Hannah kept her voice light, determined to prevent even a hint of concern from reaching her uncle's ears.

"Good, good."

There was a pause at the other end of the phone as Dawn walked past, pointing at the receiver, and mouthing, *'Who is it?'*

Hannah scribbled 'George' on the pad next to the phone, and Dawn rolled her eyes and disappeared into the kitchen.

"I hear you've got a new farmhand out there now," George continued in his stern voice.

Hannah's frown deepened. "Yes, we do." What did it have to do with her uncle? "He's a great worker and we've employed him occasionally. He's also become a friend."

There was a pause before George answered.

"I thought it my duty to remind you of your position."

Confusion filled her, and she stifled a groan. "What position? What are you talking about, Uncle George?"

"You're the owner of a farm now. Be careful, Hannah. You don't want to encourage gold-diggers."

Hannah froze, remembering her own thoughts months earlier. "Gold-diggers? Uncle George, this is the twenty-first century." Fingers of annoyance crept through her, and she took a deep breath before continuing. "I'll remember your warning. Anyway, I'm only half-owner. Any decisions relating to this farm have to be approved by Mum as well. And you know she's no fool."

"Yes, well. I thought I'd call and check that all was well and you didn't need help with anything."

Hannah resisted the urge to slam the phone down. Since when had Uncle George ever actually 'helped' on the farm? Okay, he'd maintained a close eye on the finances over the years. *But you could have done a better job so Mum and I knew Dad was struggling. If you had, I wouldn't be standing here smelling like a lavender bush now.*

"So ... do you need any assistance?"

"No thanks, Uncle George. We're fine."

"Very well then. We'll see you on Christmas Day. Goodbye."

"Bye ..." Hannah's voice trailed off, and she hung up. Christmas Day? Her heart sank as she entered the kitchen. Dawn was assembling flour, sugar, and eggs on the bench.

"Baking?"

"Yes, dear. I'll be taking some biscuits and a cake out to Ed tomorrow." She looked Hannah up and down. "And you've lost weight, Hannah. You need to eat more."

Hannah ignored her mother's comment. "You didn't mention Uncle George and Aunty Suz were coming to Christmas this year?"

"Oh." She stared at Hannah for a few seconds. "I didn't realise they were ... I mean, I had the discussion with Susan months ago but they hadn't confirmed." Dawn shrugged. "A couple extra will be welcome, anyway."

Hannah ran her fingers through her hair and re-tied her ponytail. Her uncle's words stuck in her head.

Gold-digger. Her chest swelled with indignation for a few seconds—and then she froze.

Only months ago, it was she who was finding fault with Justin, judging his intentions and condemning him before she had got to know him.

She cringed with remorse—but her uncle's warning remained with her for the rest of the day.

CHAPTER 26

The following morning, just as Tim and Jill pulled up outside, the phone rang. Hannah answered, shooing Dawn away to greet her relatives.

"Hannah. It's Otto."

"Oh, hello?"

"Delight and Pilot have had a successful joining, and your mare is ready to be collected."

"That's great news. Thank you. I-I'll be over as soon as I can."

In a dither, Hannah shared the news with Dawn and her aunt and uncle as they noisily transferred bags and a box of food into the kitchen.

Tim swept his smile around the group. "Congratulations, Hannah. We'll give you a hand to hook on the float and you can shoot over there now. We'll have a cuppa, and then your mother can take us on a tour of the lavender while we wait for you to return."

"I agree. I'm sure you can trust us to give Dawn a hand with today's harvest or whatever needs doing. You'll be home again by lunchtime, and then we can get stuck into those lambs." Jill's grey curls bobbed as she spoke.

Hannah shot them both a grateful smile. "Thanks. That'll be great. I should be back within two hours."

She grabbed the keys from the hook in the office and hurried outside, then reversed her ute out and inched backwards toward the float. Glancing in the side mirror, she smiled at Tim, signalling her with a pointed finger before holding his hand up in a stop sign.

"Thanks, Uncle Tim." Hannah pushed the seven-pin connecter plug into place and returned to the driver's seat. She flicked on the indicators, waited for the thumbs up from her uncle, then braked.

"Yep. All good. See you when you return," Tim called, and Hannah drove off.

It took fifty minutes to reach the stud as this time, Hannah knew exactly which turns to take in order to avoid holdups. Again, as she entered the property, her breath caught in wonder. Filled with brood mares, some with young foals at foot, the front paddock oozed new life while other horses stood over the hay feeders with heavy, swollen bellies.

After parking in the same spot as she did on her previous visit, she glanced around. In the arena, a group of mounted riders waited in a line, their concentration appearing to be held by an instructor. Otto? She strode toward them, halting suddenly when voices reached her from within the stable block. Recognising one as being Marie, Hannah turned toward the sound and waited while Marie hung a bridle on a hook and glanced at her.

"Hannah! I'm sorry. I didn't hear your vehicle." She turned to the girl standing beside her. "This is Claire. Claire, Hannah, Delight's owner."

The small, dark haired teenager smiled shyly and nodded. "Hi."

"Hi." She faced Marie again and smiled. "My fault. I didn't tell Otto what time I'd be here. I've missed my girl."

Marie laughed and beckoned. "Come. She's in one of the side paddocks. I'm sure she'll be pleased to go home." She walked down the row of bridles and saddles hanging on the wall and unhooked Delight's headstall.

As she trailed after her elegant host, Hannah smiled at the sight of her beautiful mare grazing contentedly on the green pasture.

"Delight! It's time to come home," Hannah called as she made her way over to the fence. A shrill whinny answered Hannah's call, and the horse trotted toward her.

"While you put her on the float, I'll fetch the paperwork," Marie said.

Delight clattered up the loading ramp, and Hannah

grinned. *Hmm, nice boyfriend, but you don't want to move in yet? I'm hearing you.*

The trip to Fantail Ridge was as swift and uneventful as the journey over and within an hour, Delight was trotting around the horse paddock, snorting, and calling for her old friends over the fence.

Hannah hung up the halter and walked thoughtfully toward the house. *Now for the next job.*

Dawn and Jill were in the kitchen as Hannah stepped inside. Jill handed Hannah a plate of sliced bread while Dawn filled the teapot.

"Perfect timing. Lunch is on the table," Dawn said.

"We've harvested the lavender that was ready for picking, and it's bunched and hanging in the drying cupboard." Jill beamed proudly.

Hannah looked at her mother, startled. "Really?" *They'd done all that.*

Dawn nodded. "Yes. I suggest we skip a couple of days now while we get these lambs done, then we should be able to manage it by cutting each morning and continuing with the rest of our chores afterward."

Tim's voice boomed from the living room, and a newspaper crackled. "I can't wait to get the first batch of dried flowers into the still. We'll pop out each week to give you a hand."

Hannah entered the living room and grinned. "Great. We'll take you up on that. I'll admit, I'm nervous—to begin with, anyway."

Tim chuckled. "Trust your old uncle. I won't let it blow up on you."

"I should hope not!" Jill's retort accompanied her look of horror as she sat down at the table. "Come on. Eat your lunch so we can get out and start on the lambs."

Hannah twisted her lips in amusement, a warm, fuzzy feeling settling within her. She shifted the cat off the dining chair and lowered him to the floor.

You two are the best aunt and uncle ever.

———

While Hannah caught and saddled Cruiser, Tim let the dogs off, and they bounced over the thick clumps of grass toward Hannah.

"I'll open the gate for you. You want the mob from the old hay paddock first, don't you?" he called.

"Yes, please!" She put her foot in the stirrup and threw her leg over the saddle with a grateful huff. Having Tim helping had already eased the pressure on her even before the job began. And the best part was that having grown up on the farm, his understanding of the process needed no discussion.

She slowed Cruiser's walk, keeping level with her uncle until they reached the gate to the sheep yards.

"Leave me to sort things out here. I'll be ready by the time you get back." He waved her away as though she were an annoying fly and she giggled, urging

Cruiser into a canter. Jet and Lass loped at her side and they covered the ground quickly, reaching the first paddock of ewes and lambs within a few minutes. At her whistles, the collie flew across the paddock, silently pushing the sheep into a tight mob while Jet loped to the farthest corner, his long strides covering the ground in seconds. Together, they ensured every animal had joined the flock before Hannah opened the gate and allowed the river of woolly bodies to flow through.

Returning to the yards was a slow, measured journey, and Hannah struggled to keep control of Jet. "Drop!" she yelled.

The enthusiastic Huntaway stared at her as though in disbelief before flopping to the ground. "Slow, I said! You're pushing them too fast."

At the front of the flock, Lass wove back and forth, desperately trying to control the leaders in her wise, well-practiced manner. Hannah shook her head. "Just as well you're such a quiet dog, Lass. Jet makes up for you both," she muttered.

By the time the sheep funnelled into the yards, Tim, Dawn, and Jill were at their posts—Tim standing beside the wide board fastened to the top of the wooden fence. The container of vaccine hung around his neck, and the castration and docking equipment was laid out in readiness. The women stood back, waiting until all ewes and lambs had passed by before they closed the gates and pushed the first lot into the catching pen, their arms flapping to keep the animals moving.

It was late afternoon when Tim wiped the sweat from his forehead. "I'll clean up here and get things ready for tomorrow. Okay, Han?" Dawn and Jill had already returned to the house to prepare a meal.

"Thanks heaps. Looks like the lambs are all back on their feet. I'll walk them to their paddock—and hopefully tomorrow, we'll get twice as many done. I'm sure Mum and I can finish the last lot on our own."

"Rubbish. We'll stay until they're finished. How many mobs did you say you've got?"

"Six." She grinned at her uncle's open mouth. "Don't worry. One lot is the Dorper lambs, and it's a small flock—and the oldest girls are a small group too, 'cause I wanted them to have a bit more feed. Anyway, they've done this so many times, I reckon we'll romp through them in half the time of the others."

"I think my price just went up—two beers per night instead of one?"

They both laughed, and Hannah mounted Cruiser and whistled the dogs.

———

TRUE TO HIS WORD, TIM RETURNED TO FANTAIL RIDGE with Jill two weeks later to supervise the processing of their first batch of dried lavender into oil. While Dawn and Hannah, and Tim and Jill stood around watching, whoops of delight filled the air when the first few drops of oil could be heard dripping into the vessel. Hannah let her breath out with a whoosh, not realising how much she had held it in until that moment.

The day after they celebrated the first batch of oil, rain broke the run of long sunny days and harvesting came to a halt. With cooler temperatures following, Hannah examined the plants each morning, a little relieved that the flowering had slowed down. *Just in time for us to enjoy Christmas—and for me to catch up with Justin.*

A wave of concern fluttered inside her. They'd both been busy. Their phone calls had been few and short, and their opportunities to get together in person even fewer. He hadn't been able to make it for the distilling process, and disappointment bit deep inside her.

It wouldn't always be like this, she reasoned. She wasn't the only one to have experienced a tough year settling into her new role. Only no matter how many excuses she made for the pair of them, she wished she could see him for more than a few minutes—perhaps even for dinner and an evening together.

After three days of rain, Hannah glanced at the calendar one dreary afternoon and frowned. "Mum, do you realise it's only a week until Christmas day?" she called out.

Dawn was stacking clean linen in the hall cupboard and didn't answer. Seconds later, she returned to the living room, carrying a large cardboard box.

"I know. It's time we put up the Christmas tree—so here it is."

Every year of Hannah's childhood, it had been a family ritual to trawl the farm plantations and select the perfect pine tree to bring home and decorate. However, while Hannah was away at university, something had changed, and she had arrived home to be greeted by an artificial tree adorned with silver and gold baubles, miniature lights, and strings of sparkling beads.

She'd been crushed and had had to bite her tongue —until her father handed her the shoe box of homemade decorations. "I'd never throw these out Han," he'd said softly.

Hannah hauled the tree out of its restraints and she and Dawn spent the next hour unpacking the battered shoe box and decorating the tree.

"Remember this one, Mum?" Hannah examined a cross-stitched candle encased in a gold frame in the shape of a dove. "Bestemor made it for me when I finished my first year at primary school."

Dawn glanced up from the pile of lights she was attempting to untangle and smiled softly. "I do remember. That was the same year she taught me to crochet." She pointed to a tiny fairy that lay in the box, her once white dress now cream and slightly lop-sided. "And that was the result."

She chuckled while Hannah continued to unpack the handmade decorations, pausing to reminisce over when and why each had been created over the years.

"I've never been this late preparing for Christmas, Hannah—and I've got no idea what to buy you." Dawn's shoulders slumped as she stepped back to plug in the string of lights that encircled the tree.

She flicked the switch and the tree twinkled with bright pin pricks of colour.

"You're not the only one, Mum. You don't need to buy me anything. Having the farm chores up to date and our first batch of lavender oil successfully distilled is enough for me."

"That would be a perfect ending to the year," she muttered while Dawn went to fetch the Christmas banners to drape across the windows.

"Did I tell you that Carol's coming up for a few days over Christmas, so I've invited her and Justin to join us?" Dawn asked.

Hannah's heart leapt.

"No, you didn't—but I was hoping Justin could come ..." Her voice trailed off, a stab of anxiety flicking through her. *Was he having second thoughts about her?* "We've both been so busy. It's ridiculous."

Dawn met Hannah's glance and raised her eyebrows. "True. There's no reason for you to have a breakdown over the work, Hannah. I worry about you."

Hannah stared at her mother, startled by the depth of concern in her voice. "I-I'm fine, Mum. Things should slow down now ... hopefully." She shrugged.

"We'd better work out what we need to cook—and buy. I haven't even thought about shopping yet, and Uncle George said they're coming. Now Carol and Justin. And, of course, Ed will be with us. Who else?"

"Tim and Jill. That's all—nine of us altogether. Let's nip into town tomorrow as soon as we've fed the animals and have a shopping spree." Excitement filled Dawn's voice and Hannah smiled.

"Good plan." And it was.

But Hannah couldn't help but think she may need to make some new plans for the new year with some different priorities—starting with herself.

CHAPTER 27

Hannah glanced down the main street. Her forehead creased at the sound of her name.

"Hannah! Dawn!" Jill hurried toward them with a lock of hair over her face and flushed cheeks. She waved madly. Reaching them, she pressed a hand against her chest and bent forward, puffing.

"Jill. What's the matter?" Dawn lay a hand on her arm and waited for her to speak.

"It's Richard. He's coming home for Christmas!"

Hannah grinned. "That's great news."

Although Richard was years older than her, there had always been a special bond between them. Fun-loving and single, he had occasionally called in at the research station when passing through Hamilton and had taken her out for lunch. She'd never quite understood what his job entailed—only that it was to do with imports of farming equipment and involved both international and domestic travel. Extroverted and enthusiastic, he was brilliant company, and Hannah looked forward to introducing him to Justin, wondering for a moment if she should introduce him as her boyfriend? Or a friend?

"Wonderful, Jill. That makes an even ten of us for Christmas day." Dawn smiled while Jill's cheeks flushed, and she lowered her voice.

"He's bringing someone home with him."

"Oh! Who?" Dawn matched her tone to Jill's as their heads drew conspiratorially close.

"Her name is Annika, and she's Swedish."

"Lovely. She'll be very welcome. Well, that's eleven of us now." Dawn drew back and glanced at Hannah. "We'd better get on with our shopping—neither of us have bought a single gift yet."

"Nor me. Oh, dear … now I'm in a bit of a quandary. What do I buy for a young woman I've never met before?" Jill's concentration had clearly shifted, and Hannah grinned.

"See you later, Aunty Jill."

"Yes, yes. I'll see you both on Christmas morning. Oh, and don't forget, Dawn, I'll bring the pavlova and fruit salad."

"Perfect," Dawn answered, and they walked along the street.

Hannah and Dawn agreed to meet back at the car in an hour, and Hannah strode up the hill, past the new clothing boutique on the way to the bookshop.

Long ago, the decision to dispense with gift-giving for the extended family had been made. Instead, they attempted to get together on Christmas Day and share good food and company. A pang of sadness swept over her as she thought of her dad and realised he would never be able to receive a Christmas gift from her again. She drew a deep breath. There was still her mother, Ed, and Justin to think about—and she wracked her brains for suitable gifts.

After pausing at the sight of a pretty dress overlaid with a soft pink scarf in the boutique's window, Hannah pushed the door open and stepped inside. It took her only minutes to choose a soft pashmina, the colour of rich sapphire, for her mother and have it gift-wrapped.

At the bookshop, she trawled through the shelves and eventually found a few gifts that she hoped would be well received. For Ed, she chose an anthology of tongue-in-cheek stories written by new citizens of New Zealand who originated from countries all around the world. For Justin, Mary Durack's *Kings in Grass Castles* and *Sons in the Saddle* seemed suitable. On one of their breaks during crutching, she remembered their brief discussion about reading and movies. At the time, she'd been a little surprised when Justin had said how much he enjoyed Australian history and the classics. She'd assumed he had gained the interest while living in the harsh outback and hoped that one day, he would share more of his experiences with her.

With the paper-wrapped books stowed in her bag, she headed back down the hill, glancing in the jewellery shop as she passed, pausing as a tiny gold clasp caught her eye. Jewellery was not something she wore much of, and on the farm, it had been impractical, saved for special outings. However, she had inherited her grandmother's brooch featuring a pair of fantails, and she loved it.

Carol. Should I get her something? She pushed the door, and a bell tinkled above her. Inside, scents of timber, polish, and the faint hint of cleaning chemicals filled the old shop, wrapping her in its warm charm.

"Hello. Can I help you?" A teenager with long dark hair asked.

"Um—yes, please. That little clasp with the fantail on it. May I have a look at it, please?"

The girl drew the tray out of the window and placed it on the counter, removing the dainty brooch from its bed of white satin. She handed it to Hannah, who scrutinized it before focusing on the price tag. Her eyes widened. It wasn't as expensive as it looked.

"I thought it would be a lot more."

A man emerged from the back of the shop and smiled at her, shaking his head. "It's not gold, only gold-plated, and very light—but pretty, don't you think?"

"Yes, I do. I'll take it, please?"

With the tiny package added to the others in her

bag, Hannah strode back to the car, a satisfied smile plastered on her face.

———

CHRISTMAS DAY DAWNED WITH STREAKS OF GOLD ACROSS the horizon. The sky quickly turned to blue, dotted with fluffy white clouds, and a soft, salty breeze drifted up from the harbour.

The flurry of cooking, cleaning silver, and preparing the house and garden for a crowd had filled both Hannah and Dawn's week. In addition to the daily farm chores, Hannah had spent an hour or two each morning harvesting and bunching lavender, and now the drying cupboard was full.

"We might do another distillation this afternoon if Uncle Tim wants to. I suspect both Justin and Bestefar will want to witness it as well," Hannah announced as she set the table.

"Good idea." Dawn rushed past, flinging the windows open before tidying up the pile of magazines on the side table. She stood with her hands on her hips and faced Hannah. "What have I forgotten?"

"Nothing, Mum. Chill. It's only nine o'clock, and you know no one will arrive before ten."

Dawn took a deep breath and nodded. "You're right. Thank goodness Justin offered to collect Ed this year." Her lips quivered, and her gaze dropped to the floor. "I miss your dad so much. He loved Christmas."

Hannah wrapped her in her arms. "I know. I miss him too." She rested her chin on her mother's shoulder and they clung together for a few moments. "I'm sure he'll be up there watching." Hannah chuckled. "I wonder what he'd think of the lavender."

Dawn held Hannah's upper arms and met her soft smile. "He'd be so proud of you."

A lump formed in Hannah's throat, rendering her speechless.

Outside, a car door slammed, and a look of horror swept across Dawn's face. She raced to the window and looked back at Hannah. "It's George and Susan."

Hannah's breath hitched, and her stomach did a leap. *Please, Uncle George, don't give Justin the third degree?*

———

THE DAY PROGRESSED WITH AN ABUNDANCE OF FOOD AND drink, together with delight and gratitude for the exchanged gifts. The roof crackled under the midday heat as Dawn ushered everyone into the dining room. Chairs scraped and glasses clinked with ice as they shuffled around the table. Hannah picked up her serviette and lay it in her lap before glancing across the table at George who appeared to be studying Justin, a frown on his face. She glared at her uncle. He held his stern expression until a flash of guilt softened his look and he turned away.

Richard and Annika appeared to have eyes only for each other, and compassion flittered through Hannah.

As soon as lunch was over, concern for Ed sobered the gathering as the old man slumped over the table, his face deathly white. Dawn escorted him to the spare room for a lie down, fussing with worry while Hannah sat on the bed beside him.

"I'm fine," he whispered. "Tired." He waved his hand weakly, as if attempting to shoo the women away. "Let me sleep."

To brighten the afternoon, Jill and Susan offered to remain in the house and monitor him while Hannah led everyone else to the shed.

"You're about to witness the distillation process of lavender oil." She waved to the still proudly. The scent of lavender already hung in the air, and she breathed it in, soaking up the pleasant smell.

She flicked the 'on' switch and stepped back. "The full process will take about half an hour," she announced proudly.

While all eyes were on the still, Justin pressed against her back, resting his hands on her shoulders and gave them a gentle squeeze. His breath was warm on her neck, and heat rose in her cheeks.

"Let's go for a walk once this is done," he whispered.

She reached up and squeezed one of his hands in response.

The thirty minutes felt more like three to Hannah as she leaned against Justin, enveloped with warmth and love. She was almost disappointed when Tim switched the engine off to cool and Richard clapped. The others joined in and a flush of pride tinged with self-consciousness filled Hannah.

"Hey Han, let's leave the oldies to have their traditional Christmas nap while we go for a walk through the bush. I've told Annika about it, and she's keen to see the fantails," Richard said. He winked at her and she grinned despite her sinking heart. It had been so long since she and Justin had had time alone, and she'd been looking forward to it.

"Sure. Come on then. Follow me," Hannah replied.

By the time they reached the bush, Hannah's fleeting annoyance had faded, her hand firmly caught in Justin's. Richard's humorous running commentary— a litany of childhood antics with Hannah and his brothers—brought smiles to their lips, and Annika's deep laugh was contagious. With Richard and Annika a few steps ahead, Justin pulled Hannah behind a large fern tree and kissed her. She clung to him, and all her work woes faded away.

"Oi. You two. Catch up!" Richard called.

Hannah giggled at Richard's command. "Merry Christmas," she whispered and pulled Justin back onto the track.

The afternoon slipped away too quickly for Hannah and, for the first time, she was envious—and resentful —of Carol. If she hadn't been staying in the cottage with Justin, it would have been Hannah who Justin might have taken home—and the thought of spending the night together filled her with feverish hope.

Ed rallied, refusing Dawn's offer to stay the night. "No. I want my home and bed." He was emphatic, and Justin and Carol obligingly installed him in the front seat of the dual cab.

"Don't worry, Dawn," Carol said. "If he needs anyone, I'll stay the night."

Before he got in his ute, Justin kissed Hannah on the lips. She grinned, aware of both mothers' gazes. *This is the twenty-first century and we're behaving like a courting couple from generations ago.*

"I'm looking after the Andersons' farm while they're away for a few days, so I probably won't get to see you until New Year's Eve. I'm looking forward to the dance." Justin stroked her arm softly, his eyes deep, chocolate pools. "Will you be my date?"

Hannah smiled. "Of course. They haven't had a dance in our community hall for years, so it should be a great night. The committee has even hired a live band."

"I'll pick you up at seven."

A brief quiver ran through her. She waved goodbye as each vehicle reversed out and drove away. Her concern over Ed eased and happiness filled her soul.

There was so much to look forward to—to live for. She gave a little skip before linking her arm with her mother's and returning to the house.

CHAPTER 28

The days dragged between Christmas and New Year's Eve, and Hannah had to force herself to concentrate on her chores. Besides the daily lavender harvest, the weeds were threatening to take over the patch again, the cattle needed shifting every three days, and with the warmer days and regular showers of rain, the lawns and hay paddocks were growing at an astonishing rate.

Hannah pulled the earmuffs over her cap and switched on the ride-on mower, relieved that her mother had at last conceded she was too tired to operate the noisy, zero-turn machine. Hannah worried about her. Dividing her energy between an acre of garden, keeping the grass under control, and helping with farm work was rapidly becoming too much for her, especially over summer when the lawns needed mowing every week and the sun beat down relentlessly.

As Hannah circumnavigated the yard, ducking under shrubs and spinning circles around the stately old trees, she allowed her mind to wander. Ellie had emailed her the week before Christmas, bubbling over with excitement about spending the break with Liam and his family at their holiday home by Lake Taupo. Apart from one short sentence asking how Justin and Dawn were, the missive covered gossip about the work Christmas party, Liam, and her family back in Ireland. Hannah had struggled to answer, unwilling to admit that she did not know what was happening with her and Justin's relationship. Instead, she simply said all was well, and that they were busy harvesting lavender.

And Justin? Well, she still didn't really know what to think. He was clearly interested in her—but where did he see their future? She wished she could see through those beautiful dark eyes and read his mind.

RACING AROUND EARLY ON NEW YEAR'S EVE, HANNAH completed the chores in record time and allowed herself a half-hour soak in the bath, filled with scented bubbles.

The peacock-blue dress she had bought to wear to Todd's work function aeons ago lay on her bed, together with the strappy sandals she had worn only once.

Fumbling with excitement, she brushed her hair

before sweeping it into a coil at the nape, allowing the wisps around her face to remain soft and loose. She threaded the dangly pearl earrings through her pierced ears and brushed another coat of mascara over her eyelashes. Last, she slipped her feet into the sandals and paraded down the hallway to her parents' bedroom.

"What do you think?"

Dawn looked up from buckling her shoes and gasped. "Oh, Hannah. You look gorgeous."

Hannah chuckled and swept her gaze over her mother's soft gold dress and beige, high-heels. "You don't look so bad yourself." *I wish Dad was here to see you all dressed up.*

Her mother fumbled with the clip of her necklace, and Hannah stepped forward and fastened it for her. "Ready?"

"Yes. If you give me a hand carrying the food to the car, I'll head off and let you wait in peace for Justin. It's a shame Carol couldn't stay for the dance—but then again, perhaps she doesn't have pleasant memories of it. To my knowledge, she only ever came to one. It was the night I met her—and the night I realised her husband, Justin's father, was not the person I thought she deserved."

Hannah stared at her mother as they walked to the kitchen. Reaching into the fridge, she passed the platters of sandwiches and pink lamington jelly cakes to

Dawn. "I didn't think of that." *Poor Carol. I wonder how she feels now, all these years later.*

Ensuring the food was safely packed in the box on the back seat, Hannah waved goodbye and returned to the house. With a stomach filled with butterflies, she busied herself with feeding Scruffy and Ragamuffin before turning on the television.

Ten minutes past seven, then twenty. Her insides were somersaulting now, and she heaved a sigh of relief at the sound of Justin's ute approaching.

"I'm so sorry I'm a bit late," he gushed. "I had to finish the milking at the Andersons' and got home less than half an hour ago."

Hannah gave him a smile, soft and understanding. "It's okay. I knew you'd come eventually." She took in his smart black trousers, pale blue shirt, and damp, freshly shampooed hair. He wore RM Williams boots on his feet—a legacy of living in Australia. "You look great."

"So do you—actually, more than that. You look absolutely gorgeous."

The butterflies settled, and she smiled widely. "So, are we right to go?"

He offered her his elbow, and they closed the back door firmly behind them.

———

Cars filled the freshly mown grass area at the front of the hall and stretched along both sides of the gravel road.

Justin parked behind a dust-covered Toyota and opened the car door for her. Hannah stepped out, thankful for the lack of rain. Her sandals were certainly not the sort of footwear that would tolerate anything but smooth, dry surfaces.

Music poured from the open doors, and Hannah's heart leapt with anticipation. The rhythmic boom of a bass drum, the clinking of glass, and the shouts of old friends and new calling greetings to each other filled the air. Justin held her hand as they walked inside, stopping to greet the throng of neighbours and acquaintances. There were so many faces Hannah didn't recognise. Presuming they were friends and family of locals come to support the district and see in the new year, she nodded and smiled at everyone they passed.

Inside, the emcee announced the next bracket of music, and Justin spun her around and put his hand on the back of her waist. "May I have the pleasure of this dance, fine lady?"

She smiled and allowed herself to be swept up in the horde of dancers, some thumping around in circles as if still wearing gumboots, and others gliding past like professional ballroom dancers. His arm tightened around her waist and she rested her right hand in his, revelling in his warm, dry grip. Beginning slowly, they had taken only a few steps before Hannah relaxed into his arms, allowing him to lead and guide her while the music—and blood, pulsed through her veins. *Man, this guy can dance too!*

The evening passed too quickly for Hannah. She introduced Justin to people he hadn't yet met, enjoyed the enormous supper, and then continued dancing for another two hours.

Dawn tapped Hannah on the shoulder. "I'm heading home, love. This is plenty late enough for me." She smiled at them both.

"We'll walk you to the car," Justin said, taking Hannah by the hand.

Dawn shook her head, frowning. "No. I'm fine and I'm parked right outside. You two stay and enjoy every minute of the evening." And before they could answer, she blended into the crowd and was gone.

At five minutes to midnight, the emcee called on everyone to join hands in an enormous circle. As the band struck up "Auld Lang Syne", the crowd moved to the middle of the circle and back out again, their joined hands raised. Everyone sang along with the music, apparently delighting in the old tradition. The count-down was joyous and deafening and, as the drum boomed the last stroke of midnight, Hannah beamed at Justin and he bent and kissed her.

In the flurry of hugs and well wishes, he drifted away and Hannah swept her gaze around the crowd, searching for him. He'd barely left her side all evening, and she suddenly felt isolated, alone—and oddly unsettled.

"Oh, there you are." She smiled at him as he turned away from the well-dressed middle-aged man who nodded politely at her. Waiting until the man moved away, she whispered, "Who was that?"

"Bill Stanton. He's the new owner of the deer farm I've been working on." His face was serious, and unease filtered through Hannah.

"Is everything alright?"

"Yes. Of course." He took her hand and shot her a small smile. "Are you ready to go home?"

Really? In the past, dancing had continued long after midnight—usually until the band refused to play anymore. She hesitated. "If you want to."

In the car, the silence was deafening as he swerved around corners and sped up across the flats at an alarming pace. Hannah's insides clenched, and the unease she'd experienced earlier deepened, spreading through her limbs like a virus.

"What's the matter, Justin?" she asked as they turned the corner near the beach and accelerated toward the homestead.

"Nothing."

Her unease morphed into disbelief. "It can't be nothing. We've had the most wonderful night—and now you can't talk to me? That's not nothing."

"I can't do it."

"Do what?"

Justin swivelled his gaze, meeting hers briefly. "Us."

"Us?" This was ridiculous. Less than half an hour ago, he was kissing her—suggesting for all the world that they were a couple. "Why? What have I done wrong?"

He shook his head. "Nothing. You've done nothing wrong. It's me—that's all."

They pulled into the Fantail Ridge yard and he got out and strode to the passenger door, reefing it open. Shock had frozen her tongue, and Hannah hauled herself out in silence.

"I'm sorry, Hannah. I can't see you again."

"What? What about if we need to hire you to help on the farm?"

He shrugged, got into the driver's seat, reversed out —and left. *What?*

Hannah stood in the yard for several minutes, unable to move. A Morepork called, reminding her she was home, and she drifted toward the gate.

The outside light glowed, throwing a pool of yellow onto the path. She slipped off her shoes and tiptoed inside.

Hannah hoped her mother would be in bed asleep. The last thing she wanted was to discuss the events of the last half hour.

She closed her bedroom door and turned on the light, staring at the pale face in the mirror. Blue eyes stared back at her, pools that sparkled with shock and unshed tears. She pulled off the earrings and reached behind her to unzip her dress. It dropped to the floor, and she glared at it for a moment before kicking it into the corner. "You're bad luck. I never want to see you again," she said in a low, fury-filled whisper. She threaded her arms into her dressing gown, turned off the light, and padded quietly to the bathroom.

Minutes later, she curled up in bed, wide awake, her head throbbing. Had she dreamed it? Why? What had happened—or what had she done that had such power to come between them? *Could he have met another woman—or have a child? Or doesn't he like me anymore?*

She rolled onto her back, her pulse racing. Too shocked to cry, she thought she would never sleep again.

———

"You were home early," Dawn said brightly.

Their eyes met as Hannah entered the kitchen, and Dawn's face dropped.

"What's happened?"

Hannah shrugged. "I wish I knew. We had the most wonderful evening. We saw the new year in and then … Justin wanted to come home. He doesn't want to see me anymore?" Her face crumpled, and she slumped into a chair, her elbows resting on the table and her hands over her eyes.

Dawn darted forward and hugged her. Stroking the

hair away from her daughter's face, she sat in the adjacent chair.

"But why? The two of you are made for each other. Carol and I have both been so delighted. What on earth could have happened?" Dawn's forehead creased, the puzzled look on her face spreading.

Hannah burst into tears. "I don't know. He wouldn't tell me—and I can't think what I've done to upset him. He's been so supportive of everything we've done here. So helpful. So kind and capable." She looked up at her mother, tears running down her face. "I really thought he was falling in love with me, and me with him. I've lain awake all night trying to work it out."

Dawn got up and marched to the bench, filled two mugs with tea, and returned to the table.

"Well. There's only one thing for it. You have a quiet day today. Go for a ride on Cruiser, have an early night tonight—and then, when you feel strong enough, you confront him. It's unfair of him to have put you in this state and not explain why."

"I can't. It hurts too much. Anyway, I don't know what to say."

Hannah swallowed the tea before dragging herself to the bedroom to dress.

She was numb. An emptiness filled her—a hollow, devoid of light. Dressed in jeans and an old shirt, she stumbled toward the stables. She had no energy to ride —or do anything that reminded her of the happiness she and Justin had shared while mustering.

Instead, she headed for the bush. Halfway down the hill, the track widened, and she stopped beside the huge tree fern where Justin had kissed her only a week before. Her legs buckled under her and she leaned back against the rough, cool trunk. She stared into the dark foliage of the bush, oblivious to the birds that flittered around her.

Hours later, she woke and blinked. A fantail was sitting on her boot and her face softened. She moved her leg, and it hopped a metre away, clearly trusting that she wouldn't hurt it. Rolling onto her knees, she hauled herself to her feet and trudged home, hunger gnawing at her stomach and her mind clearing with every step.

CHAPTER 29

The afternoon sun beat on her back the following day as Red leapt around her feet, his tongue lolling. Hannah bent and patted the dog before knocking on the door.

Her insides cramped, and she thought she might vomit as she waited for what seemed like an hour. Eventually, the door opened and Justin stood in front of her, dishevelled and dirty, as though he'd just pulled a cow from a bog. *Perhaps he had?* He clutched a mug of coffee.

"I'm not leaving until you give me some sort of explanation." Hannah held her chin up defiantly.

He stared at her for several seconds before giving a slight nod and opening the door wider.

She stepped inside and followed him to the kitchen, her arms folded and her eyes blazing. "If you say I have done nothing wrong, Justin, the least you can do is explain why you can't or won't have anything to do with me."

His shoulders slumped. "Come through. Coffee?"

"No thanks. The explanation will do."

He sighed heavily and ran a hand over his face. "I have got no money, Hannah. Well, I have savings, but nothing to match even a quarter of the value of a farm —especially your farm."

Now Hannah was even more confused. "What are you talking about?" The minute she spoke, Uncle George's warning filled her head. *Gold-digger.*

"Your family is well respected in this district—and I know as well as anyone how badly things can come unstuck if equality is not part of a successful relationship, especially in this day and age. It would be unfair of me to expect our relationship to grow and stay strong if I'm suspected of loving you for your money and not you as a person. I can't offer you what you can offer me."

Hannah snorted. "How ridiculous. I trust you, Justin. Anyway, what money? With any profits that come in going straight into the mortgage, I can barely pay the bills."

"You know what I mean. You own half of one of the nicest farms in the district and I can't afford to buy into it." He held his hand up as she opened her mouth to argue. "I've been working my backside off to save as much as I can, but it's slow going. As you know, farming is not exactly the wealthy career it once was ... so, I am trying to be fair to you."

"I think you're being ridiculous." This wasn't ideal, but at least there wasn't another woman involved—nor had an unclaimed child popped out of the woodwork.

"You can think what you like, Hannah. I'm sorry. I can't and won't ever hurt you." He rubbed his fingers through his thick hair, his voice low and strained. "Now, I need you to go."

Hannah rose and followed him to the door. They faced each other for a moment, and she thought her heart would break. Then she turned and marched to her ute, ignoring the puzzled angle of Red's head as she passed. She was too confused to be angry and the last thing she wanted was for him to see her cry.

Dawn greeted her with an anxious hug as she slammed the kitchen door. "How did it go?"

"It's all about money!" Hannah spat the words.

"Whose money?"

"Our money—or, should I say, our farm's. He said that it wouldn't be fair for us to be together because he doesn't have enough money to buy into our farm. It seems he believes in everything being equal. How old-fashioned is that!"

Dawn's face softened, and she shook her head slowly.

"Oh, Hannah. I know it's upsetting but look at things from his point of view. How would you feel?

You might think it's old-fashioned, but I think it's rather an endearing quality."

Hannah blinked and stared at her mother. She flopped into a chair, a sliver of hope flitting through her.

That's true.

———

Two weeks later, the phone rang while Hannah was ploughing through the accounts, and she picked up the handpiece absently. "Hello?"

"Hello. Is that you, Dawn?"

"No, it's Hannah."

"Oh! It's Linda here, the district nurse. I've just arrived at Ed's and I've got a bit of bad news. Is your mother there?"

"She's outside. Is it something you could tell me?"

There was a pause before Linda spoke again. "I'm sorry to have to tell you that the poor man has passed away."

Hannah groaned, holding her hand to her mouth. "Just a minute, Linda. I'll get Mum." She raced outside to where Dawn was weeding around the roses and held the phone toward her as she lay an arm around her shoulders.

"It's Linda. Ed's passed away."

Dawn's eyes widened, and she took the phone, pressing it against her ear.

"Linda?"

Dawn nodded, staring silently at Hannah as the details were being relayed to her.

"I see. Yes, certainly. I'll come now." She pressed the end button and handed the handset back to Hannah. "I'd better get cleaned up and get out there. She's rung the doctor and the undertaker, and they're both on their way."

"What can I do?" Hannah's voice quavered and Dawn hugged her, the dirt from her gardening gloves transferring to the back of Hannah's shirt.

"Nothing, love. You stay here and take care of things. I don't know how long I'll be." She stepped back and held Hannah by the shoulders. "Be strong, Hannah. He was over a hundred and has had a good life—at least since he arrived in New Zealand, anyway."

Hannah nodded and followed her mother inside, the sense of loss and emptiness deep inside her, overwhelming.

———

THE FUNERAL WAS A WEEK LATER WITH A SMALL gathering of Ed's closest friends and neighbours surrounding the graveside overlooking the harbour.

For as long as Hannah could remember, Ed had shared his love and knowledge of wildlife, the sea, and the land with anyone interested. Since he'd never learned to drive, somehow, the position of his last resting place could not have been more appropriate. There was no sign of a road and a boat rocked on the incoming tide below. Even the patch of bush behind the grave was filled with birdsong.

She linked her arm with Dawn's, thankful that Carol and Justin were facing the same direction as they did. Her heart felt as though someone had ripped it apart, and she knew she couldn't have stood any glimpse of sympathy or softening from Justin.

Back in the lounge beside the funeral parlour, a kind, middle-aged woman poured tea from an enormous teapot while her junior assistant passed around a plate of tiny savouries. Hannah shook her head and attempted a smile as the girl paused in front of her. She couldn't wait for the whole thing to be over.

Once she'd greeted all the mourners, she escaped. She hurried to the car in silence, waited for her mother to get in the passenger seat, and drove away.

All she could think of was the man who had stood on the other side of the grave, his head bowed, and his mother's arm tucked into his—and her beloved Bestefar, who now lay in peace on the hill behind them.

———

HANNAH GROANED WITH RELIEF, TOTALLY EXHAUSTED. Their first order for oil had come in the previous evening from a health shop in Hamilton, whose owner had been talking to Carol.

Thanks, Carol. You're a gem.

With the most recent cut of lavender safely dried, Dawn had combined some of it with lupin seeds to fill dozens of heat bags. A separate box sat in the corner of the living room, filled with scented bags suitable for putting amongst clothes and cupboards to ward off moths—and they packed hundreds of tiny bottles of oil into boxes waiting for labelling.

The summer had been long and hot—one of the hottest they'd experienced for years, and while it seemed to have suited the lavender, the sheep had suffered.

A quick ride around the farm earlier that morning had revealed a sheep suffering from fly-strike and Hannah was eager to nip the problem in the bud before the poor animal developed blood poisoning. It had been laying down, but when she approached, had leapt to its feet and fled. However, she had confidence that she could catch it and bring it home for treatment. Now, a storm loomed and a cool change blew in from the Tasman. The predicted rain urged her to deal with the issue before wet conditions made the job even more difficult.

She reversed Little Red out of the shed, opened the first gate, and proceeded over the farm to the ridge where she had seen the sick sheep. Pushing the throttle away from her, she urged the tractor to hurry as the band of black clouds drew closer. They chugged steadily across the paddock toward the plantation of trees her parents had planted when she was a baby, and eventually reached the spot where she'd sighted the patient earlier. At the exact moment she halted the vehicle, the clouds opened, and a deluge engulfed both Hannah and Little Red. She stepped onto the ground, wiping the rain from her eyes. Turning her collar up to prevent further rivulets from running down the back of her neck, she peered through the sheets of water. A white dot lay farther along the edge, cast in one of the sheep tracks that criss-crossed the hillside.

Hannah climbed back into the tractor and inched forward, carefully avoiding the edge of the steep slope.

The lump of dirty white increased in size as she approached. Hannah's vision was too blurry to determine if it was the sick sheep or a fallen branch from the heavily laden manuka tree nearby.

"Yes. It's yo—whoa!" A tremor rocked the ground. Not a full-blown earthquake, but a shifting beneath her. Hannah frowned, braked, and looked around. There had been no sign of birds as she'd travelled along the track beside the bush. She'd thought nothing of it. They always took shelter prior to a storm—and seemed to sense it coming well before humans did. Now, the air was silent.

Then it hit. The tractor moved and Hannah jumped off and ran, slipping in the wet grass, desperate to get away from the steep edge and onto flat ground. She turned back, horror gripping her as a chunk of the paddock broke away from the side of the slope. Like a fresh wound, it oozed watery brown blood while the earth shook. In an instant, she felt herself sliding, unable to keep her balance. As she fell, a loud crash resonated behind her. A flash of red thundered past, rolling over and over barely a metre from where she lay clinging to a tuft of long grass.

The rumbling continued, and the handful of grass loosened before giving way. The ground beneath her picked up speed. Mud filled her mouth, and the sheep somersaulted over and over in front of her.

Then her world went black.

CHAPTER 30

"Hannah! Hannah, darling. Can you hear me?"

She coughed, choking on mud as confusion filled her head. She was soaking wet, lying face down on the side of a hill with a throbbing headache. And she could have sworn she heard Justin's voice? "Justin?"

"Yes, it's me. Are you hurt?"

"I-I don't know." She tried to stand, but her feet slipped in the mud and she fell against him, clutching the front flap of his oilskin coat.

"I've got you. It's okay. Hang onto me now, and we'll crawl to the edge of the grass."

In a daze, Hannah obeyed, kneeling in the mud and holding onto his coat for dear life. Bit by bit, they worked their way from the centre of the mudslide to the firm outer edges where clumps of grass mixed with the roots of the manuka bushes.

He hauled her to a sitting position on a flat piece of

ground and wrapped her in his arms. The wind howled around them and rain lashed at her face.

"Are you hurt?" he asked again.

Hannah turned her head. "I don't think so. What happened?"

"We had an earthquake. Not a big one, but you were in the wrong place at the wrong time."

Tears filled Hannah's eyes as her purpose for being there flooded back. "The sheep? Is she …?"

Justin chuckled. "She's fine. That's her, propped against the tree over there. It stopped her fall. Don't worry about her. I'll get you into my ute and then come back for her."

"Little Red?"

"Sorry, Hannah. Little Red is no more. The tractor suffered a fatal accident and we'll have to wait until the rain's finished before we can even assess the damage or attempt to move it."

"Oh, no." Hannah let out a sob. "I was just trying to rescue the poor sheep."

Justin held her tightly, wiping the mud from her face with a gentle hand.

Hannah lifted her head and frowned. "How did you know I was here?"

"I'd just arrived back at the cottage, and I saw the storm coming. Then I saw Little Red climbing the track and worried about you—so I drove straight here." He grimaced. "Sorry about chopping up the paddocks. I didn't bother trying to stick to the tracks—just wacked her into four-wheel drive and drove across country."

Hannah barely registered his apology. He'd done all that for her. Driven all that way. Did he—did he care for her after all? "D-did you call me darling?"

He laughed. "Yes, I did. And I meant it. I love you, Hannah."

Hannah stared at him in shock. "Really? But ... you don't want to be with me?" She met his deep, worried gaze and tilted her head.

"Have you collected your mail today?" he asked.

Hannah frowned, desperate to clear the fuzziness from her head. "No. Why?"

He took both her hands in his. "When you do, I think you'll find a thick envelope full of stuff relating to Ed and his estate."

She shook her head and closed her eyes. "I'm too tired for puzzles, Justin."

"No puzzle. It's a copy of Ed's will, amongst other stuff. Apparently, besides a few different wildlife charities and organisations, you and I are Ed's beneficiaries."

Hannah opened her eyes wide. "Really?"

"Yes, really. I now have—well, soon will have— enough money to contribute an equal share and buy into your farm, if you'll have me. I want to stay here. Not just in South Head, but on Fantail Ridge. I love it— and I love you. Will you marry me?" He held her face between his hands and kissed her forehead.

She smiled, her mind wrestling with the news. "You've got mud on your lips now." She brushed a finger over them, making it worse before she answered, "I will."

"You will? Marry me?"

"Yes." She burst out laughing, a mixture of exhaustion, relief to be alive, and exhilaration sending tears down her cheeks once again.

A whiff of salt air caught in the breeze, followed by the sigh of waves as they rolled onshore.

"The winds changed, and the rain's stopped." Hannah lifted her gaze from Justin to the harbour. "Look—the leaves are falling from the trees in the plantation."

Justin took her hand in his. "New beginnings. The old makes way for the new."

She leaned against him and sighed.

"Mum's moving to Helensville. She doesn't know about Ed's will yet, but she wants to be closer to us. She's known for a long time how much I love you," he said, a soft smile on his face. "Apparently, she and Dawn have discussed their new cottage enterprise."

Hannah gaped. "What enterprise?"

He laughed. "Lavender and heat bags, lavender honey, soap, hand creams and body lotions—and, if all goes well, they're even talking of opening a café so they can sell lavender scones and ice cream."

Hannah leaned against him, and they sat in companionable silence. "Justin, it's going to be so good living here together, farming the way we want to, and never having to face problems alone."

He laughed quietly and hauled her to her feet. "I couldn't think of a more perfect life—or having a more perfect partner."

Mixed with the fresh smell of rain on the raw earth, the scent of late-flowering manuka filled the air, and a bee buzzed past. Hannah smiled at it, filled with hope and happiness. Her gaze met Justin's familiar face, his kind eyes and warm smile.

He bent and kissed her softly on the lips. "Come on. Let's go home."

And as Hannah and Justin made their way toward the homestead, she knew it had never felt as much like home as it did right then.

EPILOGUE

Hannah stared at the woman in the mirror. Was it really her? Auburn hair coiled in an elegant chignon at the nape of her neck, the veil drifting like mist from a waterfall, cascading over her shoulders and down the back of her ivory satin dress.

Dawn stood at Hannah's shoulder, a wide smile lighting up her face as she fastened the band of pearls around her daughter's neck. Alice's pearls—the beautiful necklace that Hannah's grandfather had gifted his new wife on the day of their wedding. Silver threads in Dawn's royal blue gown sparkled in the early afternoon light as she rested a hand on her daughter's shoulder.

"Ready?"

Hannah turned and met her smile.

"Absolutely".

Her gaze flicked to the photo of her father on the dressing table.

"He would be so proud of you, Hannah.'

Hannah swallowed, fighting tears that threatened to spill.

"I know", she whispered.

Six months had passed since Justin's proposal and Hannah still pinched herself to ensure that life wasn't a dream. Outside, a marque filled the area between gardens Alice had planted decades earlier and wedding guests drifted around the lawn of the homestead, chatting amongst themselves. Winter had arrived late, but the weather remained mild allowing the last of the autumn leaves to cling to the trees.

Memories of her father drifted through Hannah's mind as her insides bubbled with a mixture of excitement and sorrow that he wasn't with them. She could almost feel his arm around her–congratulating her as he planted a gentle kiss on her cheek. The shock and upset of Justin's sudden withdrawal from her after the New Year's dance had dissipated long ago. She was proud of her soon-to-be-husband's old-fashioned passion and determination in his desire to be an equal and nodded at her father's photo once again.

You would love Justin, Dad.

"Come on, Hannah. Everyone is waiting," Ellie said.

While Dawn had been putting the final touches to Hannah's veil and necklace, Ellie had hitched the deep burgundy satin dress up around her knees and dashed back and forth to the window, giving a running commentary on what was happening outside.

Hannah reached for her bouquet as Dawn linked her arm with Hannah's. They stood for a moment, facing each other, their smiles spreading.

"Thanks for everything, Mum."

Dawn gave a tiny shake of her head. "There's nothing to thank me for. If it hadn't been for you and Justin, this farm would have been sold and goodness knows where we would be now."

Hannah nodded and they made their way through the living room, pausing in the doorway. Richard hovered between the house and the marque, and Ellie gave him a thumbs up sign before smoothing her dress and fussing with Hannah's veil.

As Richard hurriedly ushered the last of the guests inside, the chatter subsided. Hannah's fluttering stomach calmed, and she took a step forward, eager for hers and Justin's special day to begin. A chord sounded from the depths of the tent before breaking into the familiar strains of Mendelssohn's wedding march.

"Come on, Hannah?" Ellie beamed at her. "It's time."

Hannah clasped her mother's hand and followed her friend to the flower-laden archway that welcomed them inside the marque.

Justin turned toward her as they entered, and Hannah smiled at him.

Their eyes locked, unwavering as she walked along the strip of red carpet and stood beside him. Hannah exchanged a soft smile with her mother as Dawn released her hand and placed it in Justin's.

His grip was warm and dry, and a calm certainty washed over her. He was her soulmate, her friend, her lover ... and now he would be her husband. Justin squeezed her hand gently, his deep brown eyes filled with adoration. A sudden recollection of her father's words many years earlier, flashed through her mind.

No matter what life throws at you, if you're with the one you love, you will always find a way through.

Her smile widened and she returned the hand-squeeze and faced the minister.

She couldn't wait for the next stage of her life to begin.

ACKNOWLEDGMENTS

I have loved writing this book—and I hope you, the reader, enjoyed reading it. There are many assistants who contribute to every book, and I am grateful to every one of you for your valuable input. Every word helps build the story–so thank you.

Special thanks go to Tim and Deborah Bonner from Aloomba Lavender Farm, Liston, NSW. I have welcomed and appreciate your guidance and valuable information about the realities of lavender farming. I can't wait until we can get together amongst the lavender.

Thank you also to Sue Trent Phillips, my lovely New Zealand friend, for your valuable knowledge in the world of New Zealand horse competitions.

To Lauren at (CREATINGInk), thank you so much for your ongoing support and professional editing skills. To Patti Roberts (Paradox Book Covers), thank you so much for your beautiful book covers, promotional graphics and more.

To my sisters, who are my constant support—thank you from the bottom of my heart. Loving appreciation goes to my husband who listens to me reading my books aloud prior to sending them to the editor, providing invaluable feedback and suggestions.

To you, dear readers, I hope you enjoy Hannah's story—the third book set on the South Kaipara Heads farm. Thank you all for reading.

ALSO BY HEATHER REYBURN

TULLAGULLA SERIES

The Cedar Tree

The English Oak

The Pepperina Grove

A Tullagulla Christmas

FANTAIL RIDGE SERIES

Peninsula Promises

The Lupin Fields

The Scent of Promise

FEATHERWOOD FALLS SERIES

A Stranger in Featherwood Falls

Secrets in Featherwood Falls

Sparks Fly in Featherwood Falls

Clouds over Featherwood Falls

Coming Home to Featherwood Falls

A Festive Featherwood Falls

OUTBACK SKYE

Letters in Blue

Dust on the Heather

The Crofter's Song

ABOUT THE AUTHOR

Born and raised in New Zealand, the highlight of Heather's childhood was the family sheep and cattle farm north of Auckland.

Reading and writing have always been a big part of family life, and from a young age, Heather dreamed of becoming a writer. With work, travel and raising a family consuming many years after settling in Queensland, it wasn't until retirement that writing became a possibility.

Heather has drawn on her love and knowledge of farming life, with more than thirty years of living on farms in Queensland's Darling Downs, fuelling her stories.

When not busy writing, Heather enjoys gardening, spending time with her family, and bush walking.

You can follow Heather on Bookbub or catch up with her via Facebook, Instagram and through her website at www.heatherreyburn.com